W9-DGM-265

Child Abuse

[OPPOSING
VIEWPOINTS®
DIGESTS]

Child Abuse

HENNY H. KIM

Greenhaven Press, Inc., San Diego, California

Library of Congress Cataloging-in-Publication Data

Kim, Henny H., 1968–
    Child Abuse / Henny H. Kim
        p.   cm. — (Opposing viewpoints digest)
    Includes bibliographical references and index.
    Summary: Presents different views on various aspects of the topic of child abuse, including defining what child abuse is, the seriousness of the problem, and ways to handle and prevent it.
    ISBN 1-56510-867-1 (lib. bdg.: alk. paper) — ISBN 1-56510-866-3 (pbk. : alk. paper)
      1. Child Abuse—United States—Juvenile literature. [1. Child abuse]
    I. Title. II. Series.
HN6626.52 .K56   2000
362.76'0973—dc21   99-047464
                                                        CIP

©2000 by Greenhaven Press, Inc.
PO Box 289009, San Diego, CA 92198-9009

Printed in the U.S.A.

CONTENTS

FOREWORD

The only way in which a human being can make some approach to knowing the whole of a subject is by hearing what can be said about it by persons of every variety of opinion and studying all modes in which it can be looked at by every character of mind. No wise man ever acquired his wisdom in any mode but this.

—John Stuart Mill

Today, young adults are inundated with a wide variety of points of view on an equally wide spectrum of subjects. Often overshadowing traditional books and newspapers as forums for these views are a host of broadcast, print, and electronic media, including television news and entertainment programs, talk shows, and commercials; radio talk shows and call-in lines; movies, home videos, and compact discs; magazines and supermarket tabloids; and the increasingly popular and influential Internet.

For teenagers, this multiplicity of sources, ideas, and opinions can be both positive and negative. On the one hand, a wealth of useful, interesting, and enlightening information is readily available virtually at their fingertips, underscoring the need for teens to recognize and consider a wide range of views besides their own. As Mark Twain put it, "It were not best that we should all think alike; it is difference of opinion that makes horse races." On the other hand, the range of opinions on a given subject is often too wide to absorb and analyze easily. Trying to keep up with, sort out, and form personal opinions from such a barrage can be daunting for anyone, let alone young people who have not yet acquired effective critical judgment skills.

Moreover, to the task of evaluating this assortment of impersonal information, many teenagers bring firsthand experience of serious and emotionally charged social and health problems, including divorce, family violence, alcoholism and drug abuse, rape, unwanted pregnancy, the spread of AIDS, and eating disorders. Teens are often forced to deal with these problems before they are capable of objective opinion based on reason and judgment. All too often,

7

teens' response to these deep personal issues is impulsive rather than carefully considered.

Greenhaven Press's Opposing Viewpoints Digests are designed to aid in examining important current issues in a way that develops critical thinking and evaluating skills. Each book presents thought-provoking argument and stimulating debate on a single issue. By examining an issue from many different points of view, readers come to realize its complexity and acknowledge the validity of opposing opinions. This insight is especially helpful in writing reports, research papers, and persuasive essays, when students must competently address common objections and controversies related to their topic. In addition, examination of the diverse mix of opinions in each volume challenges readers to question their own strongly held opinions and assumptions. While the point of such examination is not to change readers' minds, examining views that oppose their own will certainly deepen their own knowledge of the issue and help them realize exactly why they hold the opinion they do.

The Opposing Viewpoints Digests offer a number of unique features that sharpen young readers' critical thinking and reading skills. To assure an appropriate and consistent reading level for young adults, all essays in each volume are written by a single author. Each essay heavily quotes readable primary sources that are fully cited to allow for further research and documentation. Thus, primary sources are introduced in a context to enhance comprehension.

In addition, each volume includes extensive research tools. A section containing relevant source material includes interviews, excerpts from original research, and the opinions of prominent spokespersons. A "facts about" section allows students to peruse relevant facts and statistics; these statistics are also fully cited, allowing students to question and analyze the credibility of the source. Two bibliographies, one for young adults and one listing the author's sources, are also included; both are annotated to guide student research. Finally, a comprehensive index allows students to scan and locate content efficiently.

Greenhaven's Opposing Viewpoints Digests, like Greenhaven's higher level and critically acclaimed Opposing Viewpoints Series, have been developed around the concept that an awareness and appreciation for the complexity of seemingly simple issues is particularly important in a democratic society. In a democracy, the common good is often, and very appropriately, decided by open debate of widely varying views. As one of our democracy's greatest advocates, Thomas Jefferson, observed, "Difference of opinion leads to inquiry, and inquiry to truth." It is to this principle that Opposing Viewpoints Digests are dedicated.

Defining Child Abuse

In July 1995, prosecutors told a South Carolina jury how Susan Smith popped the safety brake on her car and sent it rolling down a ramp into a lake with her two boys, three-year-old Michael and fourteen-month-old Alex, strapped to carseats inside. The boys drowned that day, October 25, 1994. For the next nine days, Smith "stuck to her story about a black carjacker who commandeered the car she drove on a dark and empty back road,"[1] according to the *Detroit News*. But later it was revealed that Smith killed her two children, apparently because she was having a romantic affair with a wealthy man who had indicated that he did not want to be a father. This cold-blooded motive provoked calls for Smith's execution from a public already stunned and outraged by Smith's crime.

The Susan Smith case represents one of the high-profile stories of child abuse that have been the focus of public debate on effective responses to such heinous acts. The issue of child abuse has been at the forefront of cultural and political discussions in recent years: In the 1980s, preschool children accused daycare workers at the McMartin Preschool in California of a number of sexually abusive and bizarre acts, creating a considerable scare for working parents who left their children in someone else's care. In the 1990s, sensational stories of child abuse concerned young mothers who abandoned infants in garbage dumpsters or committed similarly atrocious acts. Overshadowed by such high-profile cases were many others that people deemed less extreme in nature.

Characteristics of Child Abuse

Incidents of child abuse appear frequently in the news, sometimes in horrifying detail. And people react to the issue of child abuse in various ways. Some tend to downplay the cases, claiming they're rare tragedies sensationalized by the media. Others conclude from just a few highly publicized cases that child abuse is epidemic. Regardless of the true incidence, it is a fact that children are physically, mentally, and emotionally vulnerable. The term *child abuse* is applied to young people up to age eighteen, although some argue that the trauma of child abuse never fades, having a lasting impact well into adulthood.

Although males and females suffer abuse in equal proportion, different groups tend to report different types of abuse. For example, the U.S. Department of Health and Human Services estimates that 77 percent of sexual abuse victims are girls and 23 percent are boys. A greater proportion of victims of medical and emotional neglect are children age eight or younger, while a greater proportion of victims of physical, sexual, and emotional abuse are children age eight or older. Economic status also plays a major role: Children from families with incomes below $15,000 a year are twenty-five times more likely to be abused or neglected than children from families with incomes above $30,000 a year.

Many people think of child abuse in terms of sensationalized stories involving predatory strangers who torture and murder helpless children. These horrific tragedies do occur. But in most incidents of child abuse the abuser is not a stranger, and in many cases the abuse is ongoing, sometimes for years. The National Committee to Prevent Child Abuse tallied 3,195,000 reports to child protective services in 1997. Of that number, over a million cases have been substantiated as actual abuse. Of the million substantiated cases, 77 percent of the abusers were the victim's parents and another 11 percent were relatives of the victim. This suggests that children are in precarious positions: They face danger at the hands of strangers but when they look toward those who are supposed to protect them—their parents—they face potentially greater danger.

Child Abuse as a Legal Issue

The attention focused on the problem of child abuse in recent years leads some people to think that child abuse is a modern phenomenon. The sad fact is that children have always been physically and emotionally abused—but only recently have legal or social definitions for their treatment been developed. Historians have shown that child abuse has existed for centuries throughout the world. Psychohistory (history of psychology) scholar Lloyd deMause has stated, "My conclusion from a lifetime of psychohistorical study of childhood and society is that the history of humanity is founded upon the abuse of children."[2] DeMause theorizes that because of their physical, mental, and emotional vulnerability, children have frequently been used as psychological "containers" into which parents have symbolically poured their own negative feelings to feel emotionally stable again. It was only in the late nineteenth century that the mistreatment of children was legally defined to provide for the basic human rights of children.

In the late nineteenth century, the United States had no laws that protected children from maltreatment. According to the New Hampshire Task Force to Prevent Child Abuse (NHTF), "Children were viewed principally as property of their parents. Legal or social intervention into family matters, no matter how cruel or harmful the family's behavior, was viewed as interference."[3] In 1874, however, the sad life of nine-year-old Mary Ellen Wilson acted as a catalyst for change in the way children were treated. After hearing repeated cries and screams from the New York City apartment where Mary Ellen lived, someone from the neighborhood alerted public health nurse Etta Wheeler, who investigated the matter.

Nurse Wheeler found Mary Ellen in a pitiful state—chained to a bedpost, the little girl was emaciated and severely bruised from frequent beatings. The nurse went to the police but discovered that there was no law to protect Mary

Ellen from her parents' absolute right to bring up their child as they saw fit. It was only after the desperate nurse begged the Society for the Prevention of Cruelty to Animals to intervene on behalf of Mary Ellen that the little girl was removed from her home under animal welfare laws. "When public attention focused on the case, the citizens of New York were shocked at the realization that the question of cruelty to animals had been regarded as more important than the prevention of cruelty to children,"[4] states NHTF. As a result, the Society for the Prevention of Cruelty to Children was established in 1875 and the general protection of children became a concern for many.

In the decades that followed, child maltreatment became an increasingly serious issue, especially for physicians who noticed a troubling pattern of mysterious injuries and frequent hospitalizations among children. In most cases doctors could not prove that parents were responsible for the injuries of these "accident-prone" children and were not aided by the few existing child abuse laws. Nearly a century later, in 1961, Dr. C. Henry Kempe collected medical and police data revealing a serious problem of child abuse, which he coined the "battered child syndrome." With mounting evidence that child abuse was a real problem, alarmed lawmakers and citizens took action to protect children's rights and ensure their safety.

How Is Child Abuse Defined?

In 1974 the federal government enacted the Child Abuse Prevention and Treatment Act, which established a legal definition of child maltreatment. As part of the act, the National Center on Child Abuse and Neglect (NCCAN) was formed to research and provide information on child abuse. NCCAN also was charged with allocating federal funds to states that establish child abuse reporting and investigation programs. As a result, every state enacted laws requiring community professionals, such as doctors and educators, to report suspected child abuse.

The Child Abuse Prevention and Treatment Act, last amended in 1996, defines child abuse and neglect as any act that results in "imminent risk of serious harm, death, serious physical or emotional harm, sexual abuse, or exploitation"[5] of a child under the age of eighteen by a parent or caretaker. Sexual abuse is narrowly defined as persuading, enticing, or forcing a child to engage in sexual activity. Child abuse is also closely linked with neglect, which implies that to fail to do something good or necessary for a child is as bad as doing something bad to a child. These federally established definitions set guidelines for the states, which maintain the authority to report, investigate, and treat child abuse cases. Specific laws for child protection vary from state to state.

Categories of Abuse

Child abuse and neglect, which are referred to collectively as child maltreatment, have been divided into four categories: physical abuse, child neglect, sexual abuse, and emotional abuse. The National Clearinghouse on Child Abuse and Neglect Information defines the four categories and establishes a context for each:

• Physical abuse means harming a child through punching, beating, kicking, biting, burning, shaking, and otherwise, regardless of whether the abuser, usually a parent or caretaker, intends to hurt the child or is carried away in "disciplining."

• Child neglect entails failing to provide for the child's basic needs, whether physical, educational, or emotional. Educational neglect, for example, includes allowing a child to miss school too many times or not enrolling the child at all.

• Sexual abuse includes fondling a child's genitals and persuading or forcing sexual activity. Sexual abuse is often considered the most underreported form of child maltreatment.

• Emotional abuse includes a parent's or caretaker's words or actions that harm a child emotionally, mentally, or socially. An example is some parents' use of harsh forms of punishment, such as locking a child in a dark closet.

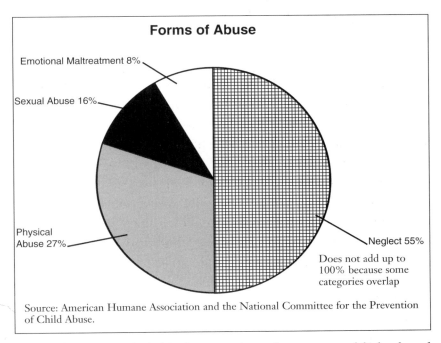

Forms of Abuse

Emotional Maltreatment 8%

Sexual Abuse 16%

Physical Abuse 27%

Neglect 55%

Does not add up to 100% because some categories overlap

Source: American Humane Association and the National Committee for the Prevention of Child Abuse.

The categories of child abuse and neglect are established and specified primarily to provide guidance to local government agencies in dealing with cases where children clearly need outside intervention. Even so, debate and legal challenges over what constitutes child abuse continue.

Whose Rights Come First?

By legally defining child abuse, the federal government decides which behaviors toward children are acceptable and which are not only unacceptable but also punishable by law, and also sets nationwide standards under which states must operate. NCCAN explains, "States must comply with the Federal child abuse and neglect guidelines to receive Federal funds."[6] Beyond that, each state establishes specific laws and services for the protection of children under its jurisdiction. All states have the legal authority to mandate reporting of suspected child abuse, refine the legal definitions of child abuse and neglect, and specify the conditions under which state agencies can intervene in family life.

Some people believe this governmental oversight of personal life is intrusive and violates individuals' right to privacy. For instance, Patrick Fagan of the Heritage Foundation argues, "Only parents can reasonably be expected to put the interests of their children above their own. Thus, government must assume that parents, not bureaucrats or politicians, are in the best position to make decisions about their children because only parents can be expected to have this overriding commitment to their children's welfare."[7] As an example of the unnecessary regulation of parent-child relationships, Fagan cites the county government of Durham, North Carolina. In 1995 the county established guidelines for identifying child abuse—which included confining an unruly child to his room—and guidelines for suitable parenting, such as being home by 9 P.M. when a twelve- to fourteen-year-old is being watched by a baby-sitter. Many feel such petty concerns are typical of the government's will to dictate the actions of adult citizens.

Others feel that the government does not intervene vigorously enough and should take a more proactive stance in protecting children from abusive parents or relatives. One sad case involved nine-year-old Rita Fisher, who was starved, savagely beaten, and eventually killed by family members. According to reporter Ulysses Currie, Rita's older sister had also been abused and removed from the home but the Maryland caseworker who investigated reports of Rita's abuse "saw no need to remove the child from her home."[8] Many viewed this tragedy as an indication that governmental agencies were incompetent in assessing child safety in the home. Programs established to remedy such inadequacies include Indiana's system of providing child welfare workers with the backgrounds of abusive parents.

Cultural Difference or Child Abuse?

People on all sides of the child abuse issue point to imprecise laws as a flaw in the system. According to legislator Bill

Backlund, today's child abuse laws have "many imprecise and vague terms" that are doing children and families "more harm than good." Backlund believes legal definitions of child abuse and neglect can be interpreted so broadly that as a result people often report any incident involving an upset child and the agencies in charge of handling child abuse cases are overburdened with the huge task of "sort[ing] fact from fiction in unsubstantiated reports."[9]

The difficulty of substantiating child abuse becomes more pronounced when religious or cultural differences figure prominently. For instance, Jeremy Leaming of the First Amendment Center reports, "A Florida couple facing criminal charges in the death of their one-month-old daughter recently asked a state judge to dismiss them, claiming their religious beliefs prevented them from seeking medical treatment."[10] The parents belonged to a religious group called the Bible Readers Fellowship, whose members refuse medical treatment because they believe modern medicine is a form of sorcery and is therefore forbidden by their religion. Although the case has yet to be settled, it has generated considerable debate over the limits of freedom of religion and official definitions of child abuse.

Another highly publicized case concerned the issue of African genital rites. A population of Somali immigrants in Houston, Texas, adhered to their ancient tradition of physically altering—the critics of the practice describe it as "mutilating"—the genitals of female children. Their Muslim faith requires this rite of responsible parents. Hence, when this African rite became a federal crime in 1996, much protest ensued about the relative definition of child abuse. As one Somali woman explains, "We [Somalis] were taught that this was a way of ensuring a girl's good behavior. It prevents them from running wild. Women should be meek, simple and quiet, not aggressive and outgoing. This is something we just accept."[11] But as far as the United States is concerned, this practice is a crime, punishable by up to five years in prison.

Is There a Solution?

Much of the data on child abuse comes from studies by governmental agencies and private research organizations. A common thread that runs through most of these studies is a tendency to focus on describing the problem of child abuse rather than on exploring ways of solving the problem. This is because although there is widespread agreement that child abuse is wrong, any plan to prevent or punish child abuse necessarily encroaches on family privacy and parents' rights. Thus, as some of the preceding examples show, the end goal of protecting children is often lost as parties argue over whose process of protecting children should be followed. Yet the questions of what constitutes child abuse and how society should deal with suspected child abusers are precisely the controversies that individuals must address as they try to help abused children.

1. Christopher Sullivan, "Jury Rejects Death Penalty for Susan Smith," *Detroit News*, July 29, 1995, http://detnews.com/menu/stories/12189.htm.

2. Lloyd deMause, "The History of Child Abuse," presented as a speech before the British Psychoanalytic Society in London, 1993, www.geocities.com/HotSprings/Spa/7173/ph-abuse.htm.

3. New Hampshire Task Force to Prevent Child Abuse, "A Short History of Child Abuse," *Resources*, July 16, 1998, www.gran-net.com/nhtf/res-history.htm.

4. New Hampshire Task Force to Prevent Child Abuse, "A Short History of Child Abuse."

5. Quoted in National Clearinghouse on Child Abuse and Neglect Information, "What Is Child Maltreatment?" February 25, 1999, www.calib.com/nccanch/pubs/whatis.html.

6. National Center on Child Abuse and Neglect, *A Coordinated Response to Child Abuse and Neglect: A Basic Manual.* Washington, DC: U.S. Department of Health and Human Services, 1992.

7. Patrick F. Fagan, "How Congress Can Protect the Rights of Parents to Raise Their Children," *Heritage Foundation Issues Bulletin*, July 23, 1996, www.heritage.org/library/categories/family/ib227.html.

8. Ulysses Currie, "Protection for Maryland's Most Vulnerable," *Washington Post*, May 16, 1999.

9. Bill Backlund, "Imprecise Child Abuse Laws Do More Harm than Good," *Northwest News*, August 25, 1998, www.comzone.com/nwnews/nnissues/v16n16/ed2.html.

10. Jeremy Leaming, "Parents Ask Florida Court to Dismiss Child-Abuse Charges," *Free!* October 27, 1998, www.freedomforum.org/religion/1998/10/27childabuse.asp.

11. Quoted in Celia W. Dugger, "Tug of Taboos: African Genital Rite vs. American Law," *New York Times*, December 28, 1996.

CHAPTER 1

How Serious Is the Problem of Child Abuse?

"Far too often, people suspect child abuse but don't report it because they feel it is 'none of their business.'"

Child Abuse Is Seriously Underreported

Child abuse takes many different forms. A little boy, beaten by his frustrated mother, bears bruises on his body but denies that his mother ever touched him. A baby in the care of foster parents ends up in the emergency room with traumatic injuries for which no one will take responsibility. A young girl appears terrified to be alone with an adult male cousin who has sexually molested her and threatened her to keep the incident a secret.

Stories like these seem to appear in the news almost every day. Approximately 2,000 children die from physical abuse and neglect each year, according to the National Center for the Prosecution of Child Abuse. The National Committee to Prevent Child Abuse reports that 1,054,000 cases of child abuse have been confirmed by child protection services. Yet these figures do not reflect the true extent of the problem. It is difficult to discern just how many incidents of child abuse go unreported, simply because statistics are based only on reported cases. What is evident is that many—probably most—incidents of child abuse are not reported, both because children tend to keep their abuse secret and because uninvolved adults too often ignore or deny the problem.

Only the Most Severe Physical Abuse Is Reported

The main reason child abuse is underreported is that it often occurs in the home—in private settings where a powerless child's cries for help cannot be heard—and thus it can be hard to detect. Once outside the family, the child often feels too frightened or ashamed to reveal that he has suffered at the hands of the people who are supposed to protect and care for him.

Abused children are often coached to repeat made-up stories about their "clumsiness" and threatened into covering up the abuse altogether. One abused child may pretend not to know how she got such large bruises on her body; another child with a black eye may claim he accidentally ran into a door. And yet the signs of physical abuse—the actual scars on the child's body—cannot be denied. Unfortunately, only the appearance of physical scars can provide a concrete means of determining that abuse has occurred and from this determination the offender can be prosecuted. Because physical abuse has led to the death of many innocent children, using physical wounds as evidence of child abuse can save a child's life, since many abused children ultimately die, directly or indirectly, from abuse inflicted on them by their own parents.

Unfortunately, the persons best in the position to report these signs of abuse—physicians—are often reluctant to do so. Some feel that child protection services are too rash in separating children from parents in suspected but unproved cases. Others are simply insensitive to these children's pain. According to one investigator, "Some physicians find reporting inconvenient, begrudging not only the hours they might have to spend in court testifying but also the time to make the initial call or write a report."[1] Such insensitivity is not the norm but does exist and, sadly, leads physicians to go about their jobs without remorse for blatantly ignoring a child's need.

Sexual Abuse Leaves No Easily Identifiable Physical Scars

Moreover, not all types of child abuse leave easily identifiable scars. Although sexual abuse is another form of physical abuse, it is more difficult to gather physical evidence for this problem. According to the Center for Children in Crisis, "Often these child-victims communicate their pain and suffering silently through their behavior or in the sad, vacant stare in their eyes."[2] Sexual abuse, which involves "forcing, tricking, bribing, threatening, or pressuring a child into sexual awareness or activity,"[3] makes up at least 8 percent of the reported cases of child abuse, according to the Sexual Assault Crisis Center.

The Center for Children in Crisis estimates that every hour seventeen children are sexually abused in the United States. Yet most authorities agree that sexual abuse is vastly underreported. The Sexual Assault Crisis Center reports that in 70 to 85 percent of the cases, children are sexually abused "by someone they know and trust: a relative, family friend or caretaker."[4] Given the conflicting mix of familiar surroundings with unfamiliar behavior, children feel confused about what is happening to them and helpless to stop the actions of a familiar authority figure. In particular, the sexual abuse of boys is most likely to go unreported, according to a study published by the *Journal of the American Medical Association*. Dr. William Holmes of the University of Pennsylvania School of Medicine explains, "Abuse of boys has not been well documented, in part because boys fear they won't be believed or will be labeled homosexual."[5] Dr. Marjorie Hogan, a pediatrician in Minneapolis, Minnesota, notes that only a fifth of reported cases involve boys, a serious concern: "It's such a secret crime and the way we gather information is fraught with problems. I think the numbers are far higher than we think."[6]

Children Are Powerless

Children are frequent victims of abuse by parents, relatives, and strangers simply because they are by nature almost helpless. Their small physical size limits their ability to fight back when assaulted by an adult. In addition, children are dependent on their parents for physical, mental, and emotional nourishment, and often stripped of the power to speak up or reveal their own feelings. They are not aware that they have rights as individuals apart from their parents, including the right not to be sexually or physically abused. If the abuser is a parent, the child probably has too much fear and not enough information to know that this parent should be reported to the authorities.

Reporting a parent for sexual or physical abuse is often not an option for a child because the parent is seen as the ultimate authority figure. The child is not likely to challenge the actions of the most powerful person in that child's world. Children often do not understand what is happening to them or are unable to describe their experiences because of the emotional trauma that comes with physical or sexual abuse. Another reason why children keep quiet is that the abusing parent may control the child with threats or lies, preying on the child's fear and shame.

Children feel shame at being abused by their parents because they instinctively know that it is wrong. They may blame themselves for being unable to stop the parent from performing such hurtful acts. Abused children's shame also comes from knowing that society attaches a considerable amount of stigma to child abuse, particularly to sexual abuse. Incest, or sexual abuse within families, is considered highly taboo. The abused child fears the consequences of having the abusive parent's actions revealed and, perhaps even more, being considered abnormal or damaged.

A Lack of Intervention

Parents who abuse their children obviously have emotional or mental problems, and certainly aren't about to report their own crimes to the authorities or get the psychological help necessary to stop their abnormal behavior. Thus, society cannot rely on the abuser or the victim to report incidents of child abuse. If the problem of child abuse is to be confronted, the underreporting has to stop, which means that outsiders must take part in the effort.

Outside adults are in the best position to notify the authorities of the possibility of child abuse. But far too often, people suspect child abuse but don't report it because they feel it is "none of their business" or they fear challenging another parent's parental authority. This misguided respect for "family privacy" is the main reason that child abuse goes unreported. If an individual truly cares about the plight of abused children, then he or she should not hesitate to report a suspected child abuser. Adults should feel it is their social responsibility to report possible child abuse. Unfortunately, this is often not the case.

Many adults deliberately overlook obvious signs of child abuse. Fear of retaliation from the abusing parent is a major reason why other adults are reluctant to get involved. Another reason is that many ordinary people, feeling too uncomfortable with the realities surrounding such inappropriate treatment of children, pretend not to notice the telltale signs of child abuse. They take the cowardly route of denying that the troubling situation exists at all, doing nothing to put a stop to the abuse, and allowing the child's suffering to continue. When adults shirk their social responsibilities through denial and passivity, they are, in effect, allowing another innocent child to stay imprisoned in suffering and making the seriously underreported problem of child abuse worse, not better.

1. Janice Somerville, "More Harm than Good," *American Medical News*, January 6, 1992, p. 99.

2. Center for Children in Crisis, "Incest: The Ultimate Betrayal," March 25, 1998, www.shadow.net/~cpt/.

3. Sexual Assault Crisis Center of Knoxville, TN, "Child Sexual Abuse," May 27, 1996, www.cs.utk.edu/~bartley/sacc/childAbuse.html.

4. Sexual Assault Crisis Center of Knoxville, TN, "Child Sexual Abuse."

5. Quoted in MSNBC News Services, "Sexual Abuse of Boys Underreported," March 11, 1999, www.msnbc.com/news/219683.asp#BODY.

6. Quoted in MSNBC News Services, "Sexual Abuse of Boys Underreported."

"The actual number of children found to be abused is 15 out of every 1,000 reported cases, certainly no indication that child abuse is epidemic."

The Prevalence of Child Abuse Is Exaggerated

No one can dispute the fact that child abuse is a serious problem. Whether it concerns one innocent child or thousands, child abuse cannot be dismissed or taken lightly. But an increasing irrational paranoia is threatening to trivialize the issue of child abuse by changing the definition of the term. This redefinition may compromise the serious weight that child abuse has traditionally carried in society.

Inflated statistics and media-generated hysteria surrounding just a few notorious child abuse cases have created the inaccurate perception that child abuse is rampant. Acting on this unfounded belief, even well-intentioned citizens end up wasting the resources of the child protection services, the time and money that could have helped a needy child. In the long run, suspicion and paranoia harm because they hinder careful investigations and prevent effective solutions for actual incidents of abuse.

Statistics in Perspective

With each sensationalized story, the media adds to the belief that physical and sexual abuse of children has suddenly surged in the last decade of the twentieth century. This perception's inaccuracy is shown through careful examination of the numbers. The National Committee to Prevent Child Abuse reports that in 1997 over 3 million incidents of child abuse and neglect were reported to child protection service agencies. Apparently, this number is a 41 percent increase from the 1988 numbers, which experts attribute to a "greater public awareness of and willingness to report child maltreatment, as well as changes in how states collected or defined a reportable act of maltreatment."[1]

Three million maltreated children is certainly an alarming number, but this statistic is misleading. It indicates the number of reports the agency received to investigate *possible* incidents of abuse or neglect, not the actual number of children found to be abused. The actual number of children found to be abused is 15 out of every 1,000 reported cases, certainly no indication that child abuse is epidemic.

In reality, the number of cases of *actual* abuse has decreased. The National Committee to Prevent Child Abuse provides evidence:

> According to the 1997 survey, physical abuse represented 22% of confirmed cases, sexual abuse 8%, neglect 54%, emotional maltreatment 4% and other forms of maltreatment 12%. These percentages have undergone some shift since 1986 when approximately 26% of the children were reported for physical abuse, 16% for sexual abuse, 55% for neglect, and 8% for emotional maltreatment.[2]

The numbers reveal that within ten years there has been a shift from previous reporting categories to the newly designated category, "other forms of maltreatment." The addition of the abstract category "other forms of maltreatment" reveals the fluctuating definition of child abuse, a change that does less to provide immediate help for abused children and more to generate confusion as the debate over what constitutes child abuse takes precedence over action.

The Expanding Definition of Child Abuse

Statistics are frequently used to support claims of the rapid rise of child abuse. But the statistics used by researchers in investigating child abuse are not always reliable. In fact, with so many different studies revealing differing numbers, it is difficult to decide which is accurate. According to psychologist Jim Hopper, "The most controversial issues [in statistical studies] are how to define abuse . . . and which definitions are applied to research data."[3] Different studies employ techniques based on different definitions of child abuse. As a result, there is no real body of evidence to suggest that child abuse is everywhere.

More prevalent than the actual occurrence of child abuse is the paranoia generated by the loosened definition of child abuse. The term "child abuse" seems to have lost its real meaning; now, many nonphysical exchanges between an adult and a child can be considered child abuse. For example, some consider yelling at a child for misbehaving to be child abuse—on par with physical injury and sexual molestation. This in itself is a ridiculous abuse of the term, since yelling is clearly not physical or sexual abuse. A federal legislation's definition of child neglect, which includes "marked inattention to the child's needs for affection," is made even more abstract: "The assessment of child neglect requires consideration of cultural values and standards of care."[4] Such abstract definitions ultimately give child protection services the power to decide what constitutes child abuse and what can be attributed to "cultural values."

Conscientious parents can be made to feel extremely self-conscious, if not defensive, about the way they rear their children because the general sentiment of society has moved from allowing parents to use their personal judgment for raising children to insisting parents abide by popular notions of proper parental behavior. For example, spanking was once considered a standard means of disciplining a child and was rarely questioned. A good, moral parent was entrusted to use spanking as a tool to teach her children right from wrong, which worked, as evidenced in the number of spanked children who grew up to be responsible adults. Now the tool is under scrutiny.

Paranoia and False Accusations

With the growing hysteria, society's trust in individual morality has eroded and parents' methods of rearing their children have become everybody's business. Now it seems that everyone else—those not responsible for raising the child—criticizes the use of spanking. Outsiders interfere in the lives of reasonable adults by carelessly accusing the disciplinary parent of physical abuse. Ironically, if a parent decides against spanking, the child is likely to develop into a troublemaker, the kind of "delinquent" who supposedly resulted from poor parenting. Perhaps only then will it become clear that proper

parenting involves the utilization of spanking. For now, however, misinformation and shortsightedness perpetuate the idea that spanking equals child abuse.

In today's suspicious society, almost anything a parent does—or does not do—may be considered abusive. Just one call from an outsider can bring in the child protection services, which can summarily separate innocent parents from their helpless children. "In rightly seeking to identify cases of child abuse, some people can be overzealous, catching innocent and unsuspecting parents and other caregivers in a complicated net of officialdom,"[5] according to *Moms Online*, an online parenting publication. The prospect of such complications creates psychological stress for parents and their children.

Children Can Be Confused

Children who are not abused can still be caught up in child abuse hysteria. The media, eager to jump on a scandalous story, often turns one tragic incident into a frightening epidemic. In the mid-1980s, a notorious case of child abuse at the McMartin Preschool, a daycare center in California, was sensationalized by news agencies across the country. "Such publicity has created the perception that abuse is commonplace in these out-of-home settings,"[6] states the National Committee to Prevent Child Abuse. As a result, all daycare centers came under suspicion, warping the thinking of children and their parents.

One sad result of this hysteria was the case of San Diego Sunday school teacher Dale Akiki, whom nine children accused of rape, sodomy, and torture. Immediately, the accused was assumed guilty before he had a chance to prove his innocence. At the court hearings, the children voiced ridiculous claims that the teacher killed a baby and slaughtered an elephant and a giraffe. Journalist Hans Sebald reports that "The jury in the Superior Court concluded that the children weren't credible and acquitted Akiki,"[7] but this was only after the innocent man had spent nearly three years in jail.

Clearly, the inaccurate perception that child abuse is prevalent can be harmful. Parental rights can be taken away and adults can be falsely accused of child abuse. Innocent children are being taught to be suspicious and sometimes to harm others with a distorted view of reality. Even more harmful, the exaggerated notion that child abuse is prevalent takes much-needed attention away from the real task at hand, which is to arrive at concrete solutions for helping those children who actually have been abused. Better ways to make the world safer for children and adults include remaining rational in a time of hysteria, utilizing careful judgment in examining studies, and keeping a watchful eye out for real signs of abuse instead of allowing that vision to be obscured by misinformation and sensationalism.

1. C.T. Wang and D. Daro, *Current Trends in Child Abuse Reporting and Fatalities: The Results of the 1997 Annual Fifty State Survey.* Chicago: Prevent Child Abuse America, 1998.

2. National Committee to Prevent Child Abuse, "Child Abuse and Neglect Statistics," April 1998, www.childabuse.org/facts97.html.

3. Jim Hopper, "Child Abuse: Statistics, Research, and Resources," July 24, 1998, www.jimhopper.com/abstats.

4. National Clearinghouse on Child Abuse and Neglect Information, "What Is Child Maltreatment?" February 25, 1999, www.calib.com/nccanch/pubs/whatis.htm.

5. Moms Online, "Child Abuse and Neglect," March 5, 1998, www.momsonline.com.

6. National Committee to Prevent Child Abuse, "Child Abuse and Neglect Statistics."

7. Hans Sebald, "Witch-Children: The Myth of the Innocent Child," *Issues in Child Abuse Accusations,* vol. 9, no. 3/4, Summer/Fall 1996, p. 180.

"Given the hostility of a society in denial, adults who declare their recovered memories of abuse have made the courageous decision to confront the ugly truth of child abuse."

Claims of Child Abuse Are Usually Valid

Claims of child abuse must be taken seriously if society is to move toward providing children with the basic human rights that adults take for granted. If a child reveals that he or she has been subjected to abuse, immediate action toward intervention must be taken. And when an adult recovers suppressed memories of being abused as a child, the situation must be taken seriously because the harm done to innocent people has never been addressed. Overall, claims of child abuse deserve full attention and action from the community. Attempts to invalidate child abuse claims will only ensure that the pervasive problem continues to be ignored.

If a child claims that he has been physically assaulted or sexually molested by an adult—a daycare provider, a neighbor, or even a parent—he is probably telling the truth. Innocent children are incapable of creating such disturbing accounts, whose gruesome details seem right out of an adult horror novel. Additionally, children already fear retaliation from adults, all of whom have physical and social power over them. It is highly unlikely that a child would deliberately put himself at risk by revealing the identity of the offender, unless the fearful child is desperate enough to seek help.

Children Make Good Witnesses

In truth, children live in dangerous situations, a fact that many adults choose to overlook. Claims of child abuse threaten to confront adults with an ugly reality and force them to respond. Adults often avoid confronting the terrible truth by imagining that the child is making up stories. But Dr. Carolyn Newberger, an expert on sexual abuse, says that children are likelier to lie by denying something that really happened than by making something up that never occurred. "That would indicate there are far more children who are abused and don't let anyone know than who are not abused and tell someone they are,"[1] says Dr. Newberger.

When children reveal that they have been abused, they often are not believed. This has terrible consequences in that children learn that honesty does not count for much in the adult world. Additionally, the child whose own account is invalidated may become confused about what actually has happened. This may imply to children that they do not possess the ability to perceive reality accurately. Skeptical adults have assumed that children are often coached into claiming they've been abused for the purpose of granting one parent sole custody of a child of divorce. However, this popular view has been proven wrong. The American Psychological Association states that "some professionals assume that accusations of physical or sexual abuse of children that arise during divorce or custody disputes are likely to be false, but the empirical research to date shows no such increase in false reporting at that time."[2]

Others seem to assume that children do not possess the mental or emotional capacity to describe their experiences accurately. Studies have shown this to be untrue. For instance, the National Institute of Child Health and Human Development thoroughly examined the accuracy of one child's account of sexual assault. The study recorded the child's accounts in various clinical settings and then examined the consistencies and inconsistencies in the accounts. The organization found that "children can indeed provide remarkably detailed and accurate accounts of their experiences."[3]

Another study, by psychology professor Carol Peterson, revealed that children remember quite well what happened to them in traumatic events. Peterson interviewed more than two hundred children after they had been brought to the emergency room for physical injuries and then again, six months after their injuries. "We were surprised at how much the children remembered," said Peterson. "Two-year-olds only remembered about half of the important information, but by three years of age children remembered most of the event."[4] By age three, children made very few mistakes in recalling the circumstances of their injuries.

Children Face Many Obstacles

Even when a child reports an adult abuser, action cannot necessarily be taken without legal intervention. This means that the child must act as her own witness, which often can be traumatic, especially if the child must testify against her own mother or father. Compounding the child's trauma is the fact that, as attorney Sylvia Gillotte reveals, "historically, children have been perceived as unreliable, unbelievable, and unable to distinguish between fact and fiction."[5] In a sense, the already fearful child is penalized further with the assumption that only adults can accurately depict reality. This assumption grants adults further control in a situation where the child is already at a disadvantage.

The child's disadvantage—the denial of his or her credibility—has been relieved somewhat by the development of strong, consistent guidelines to be used by professionals in helping children discuss their abuse in ways that are believable or make sense in the adult world. For example, the Office of Juvenile Justice and Delinquency Prevention established its child-witness interviewing guide with the understanding that although children do not express themselves in the same way adults do, they still can accurately describe their experiences. Investigators are advised to ask direct, concrete questions the child can understand and to be sensitive to the child's level of development.

The Office of Juvenile Justice and Delinquency Prevention holds that "children can provide accurate information that is meaningful to an investigation if asked direct questions about central aspects of the event."[6] Investigators should focus on being objective and avoid using leading questions, according to the guide. With an accepting, unbiased environment, children can accurately describe their situations to those in the position to intervene and provide positive change. Unfortunately, many children never experience that kind of positive environment.

Memories of Child Abuse May Not Surface Until Adulthood

Children who have never been able to speak out about their abuse often hide their pain from society and even from themselves. Feeling overwhelmed by their trauma, children sometimes react psychologically by forgetting about painful incidents. Years or even decades later, when an adult enters therapy for emotional problems, the painful memories are finally recalled.

However, just as critics believe that children can be coached into making up stories of abuse, they believe that some adults possess equally impressionable minds that are manipulated by professionals. Hence, when adults remember being abused as children, skeptics invalidate the recovered memories as the result of imaginative therapists and weak-minded patients. "The notion that therapists can implant scenarios of horror in the minds of their patients is easily accepted because it appeals to common prejudices,"[7] explain Judith Herman and Mary Harvey, directors of a program called Victims of Violence. Common prejudices include the notion that child abuse is not

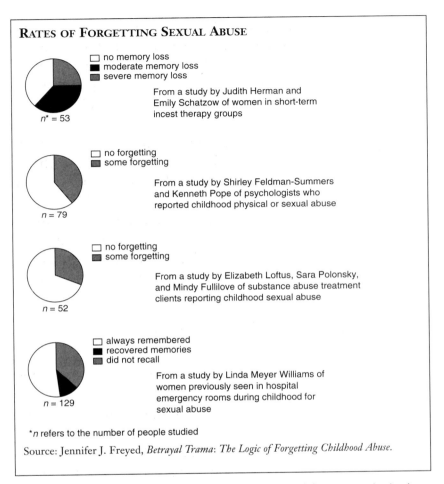

RATES OF FORGETTING SEXUAL ABUSE

☐ no memory loss
■ moderate memory loss
▨ severe memory loss

From a study by Judith Herman and Emily Schatzow of women in short-term incest therapy groups

n* = 53

☐ no forgetting
▨ some forgetting

From a study by Shirley Feldman-Summers and Kenneth Pope of psychologists who reported childhood physical or sexual abuse

n = 79

☐ no forgetting
▨ some forgetting

From a study by Elizabeth Loftus, Sara Polonsky, and Mindy Fullilove of substance abuse treatment clients reporting childhood sexual abuse

n = 52

☐ always remembered
■ recovered memories
▨ did not recall

From a study by Linda Meyer Williams of women previously seen in hospital emergency rooms during childhood for sexual abuse

n = 129

*n refers to the number of people studied

Source: Jennifer J. Freyed, *Betrayal Trama: The Logic of Forgetting Childhood Abuse.*

prevalent and that people exaggerate or fabricate victimization. Relying on this prejudice brings comfort to people who are reluctant to confront the difficult situation of child abuse. By accusing victims of lying about being abused, skeptics can continue to deny that child abuse is a big problem.

Given the hostility of a society in denial, adults who declare their recovered memories of abuse have made the courageous decision to confront the ugly truth of child abuse. No sane adult would claim his parents abused him as a child, tearing apart his family and bringing considerable pain to everyone involved, unless it was actually true and the adult felt no choice but to confront the terrible thing that happened to him as a child. Adults, such as Sharon Simone, a public educator, speak out at the cost of considerable personal pain because they want to break the cycle of child abuse, secrecy, and denial.

Recovered Memories Are Valid

Simone spent ten years dealing with memories of abuse that came to her nearly thirty years after she'd experienced them. She continued to be haunted by her traumatic experiences: "I am remembering the dangers: Dad coming into my bedroom at night; him hitting us; Mom letting him. My shaking for years as I remembered those events in my forties and the long, dark underworld that was my childhood."[8] Simone and her sister won a civil suit against their father, a former FBI agent and well-known child abuse educator, but this victory cost her closeness with family members, who were angry at having their secret revealed to the public. But eventually, her father admitted his guilt and Simone was able to forgive him, as well as show her own son that the cycle of abuse could be broken.

Just as legal action is available to children who claim abuse, it is accessible to adults who remember being abused as children. "Because most child victims do not disclose sexual abuse while they remain under the authority of their abusers, some states have extended their statutes of limitation to allow adult survivors legal redress,"[9] according to Herman and Harvey of the Victims of Violence program. This is an important factor in beginning to heal the pain that child abuse causes. In the long run, if society dares to confront the problem of child abuse, the children and adults who have experienced the worst aspects of the problem must be believed.

1. Quoted in Carey Goldberg, "Getting to the Truth in Child Abuse Cases: New Methods," *New York Times*, September 8, 1998.
2. Quoted in Sherry A. Quirk, "When Children Tell and No One Listens," *Facing the Issues: Grief and Mourning*, July 12, 1997, www.yesican.org/articles/childrentell.html.

3. Yael Orbach and Michael E. Lamb, "Assessing the Accuracy of a Child's Account of Sexual Abuse: A Case Study," *Child Abuse & Neglect*, January 1999, p. 96.

4. Quoted in Tammy Hardiman, "Research Asks: Just How Reliable Are Children's Memories," *Memorial University of Newfoundland Gazette*, April 25, 1996, www.mun.ca/univrel/gazette/1995-96/April.25/or1-asks.html.

5. Sylvia Lynn Gillotte, "The Child Witness," *Representing Children in Family Court: A Resource Manual for Attorneys and Guardians ad Litem*, published by the South Carolina Bar, November 4, 1997, www.childlaw.law.sc.edu/resourcemanual.

6. Office of Juvenile Justice and Delinquency Prevention, *Interviewing Child Witnesses and Victims of Sexual Abuse*. Washington, DC: Office of Juvenile Justice and Delinquency Prevention, 1996.

7. Judith L. Herman and Mary R. Harvey, "The False Memory Debate: Social Science or Social Backlash?" *Harvard Mental Health Letter*, April 1993, www.mentalhealth.com/mag1/p5h-mem3.html.

8. Sharon Simone, "Salem, Massachusetts 'Day of Contrition,'" *Facing the Issues: Grief and Mourning*, January 14, 1997, www.yesican.org/articles/salem.html.

9. Herman and Harvey, "The False Memory Debate."

"Irrational thinking distorts ordinary details—a mere diaper rash might be interpreted as a sign of sexual abuse, and the lives of decent people can be altered drastically."

Claims of Child Abuse Are Often False

Any claim of child abuse requires serious consideration. Yet a rigid belief in the complete veracity of the alleged victim's claims sometimes creates new victims of the falsely accused. The truth is that child abuse is a big problem. But this problem is hardly combated by the prevalence of child abuse claims that turn out to be false. If anything, the problem is made worse by generating hysteria that creates suspicion and prevents people from acting together to protect innocent children, as well as adults.

Children Have Lied Before

History has shown that children are not immune to harmful acts against others. A prime example of this is the Salem witch trials. The trials, held in Salem, Massachusetts, in 1692, resulted from the lies told by the town's children, accusing various adults of being witches. The children's invented stories generated so much hysteria in the town that every adult feared accusation. Eventually, twenty people were executed as witches. This atmosphere of irrationality and its victimization of innocent people are not limited to the historical incident in Salem. In fact, they have been re-created again and again, at various times and in different contexts.

Sociology professor Hans Sebald cites expert opinion that "children have an incomplete grasp of the contours of the real world and often resort to making up stories if they are under pressure or if they sense that such stories are expected."[1] Some children make up stories to get their parents' attention or to cause outsiders to feel sorry for them. Others—especially those who claim that a parent is the abuser—simply act under the influence of other adults. Manipulative adults often use children and their highly suggestible states to benefit themselves in legal situations.

Parents Use False Claims Against Each Other

A primary exploitation of children's suggestibility is in the realm of child custody. In his essay "A System Out of Control: The Epidemic of False Allegations of Child Abuse," Armin A. Brott reports a troubling trend in which parents use their children as weapons in divorce and custody struggles. Brott reports that the number of false allegations of child abuse in divorce cases has surged in the 1990s and estimates that 75 to 80 percent of the allegations are completely false.

"Several studies have shown that women who deliberately make false allegations are obsessed with hurting their husbands as much as possible,"[2] says Brott, who also notes that 95 percent of parents who level accusations of child abuse against a former partner are women. Such devious parents attempt to brainwash their children into believing they've been abused by the targeted parent, and then seek out professionals—doctors, lawyers, and therapists—who can validate the invented abuse.

Columnist Martin Galloway, a single father who once faced grueling evaluations from his ex-wife's lawyers and court mediators, claims that some overzealous battered women's shelters recommend tactics to invent a child abuse situation. The point is to cause the father to be investigated by overeager child welfare agencies, which usually works against the father. The devious tactics include shopping around for a therapist willing to report child abuse and repeatedly taking the child for physical examinations to organizations that will alert child welfare agencies.

Overeager or inexperienced child welfare workers often ask children leading questions or confuse them into lying about abuse that never happened. Says Galloway, "What child abuse professionals have recently found is that they could get just about any child to make an abuse disclosure. Using highly suggestive questions, interviewing techniques and anatomical dolls (now discredited), they could easily implant false memories in any young child."[3] But overzealous child welfare workers are not necessarily the major factor in creating a climate of paranoia about child abuse.

During stressful events such as divorce, everyone involved can be influenced in one way or the other by the notion that child abuse is a factor. There is already a public perception that child abuse is rampant in modern society. Hence, parents grow suspicious of each other, intermediaries enter the situation with preconceived notions of abuse, and even children begin to think they've experienced things they haven't. Irrational thinking distorts ordinary details—a mere diaper rash might be interpreted as a sign of sexual abuse, and the lives of decent people can be altered drastically. Like the Salem witch trials, lies and suspicion grow into hysteria and innocent people are accused of being child molesters, which today carries as much of a stigma as witchcraft did centuries ago.

Recovered Memories Create Pain

The hysteria of false allegations has given way to another troublesome phenomenon: recovered memories. "Long-repressed memories that emerge after decades, often during psychotherapy, have become food for our hungry mass media,"[4] says psychology professor Elizabeth Loftus. Many adults believe that overwhelmingly painful childhood experiences are repressed and forgotten until the child becomes an adult and enters therapy for emotional or mental problems.

The testimonies of well-known celebrities, such as Roseanne Barr, recounting the discovery of their own abuse have created a perception in the general public that sexual abuse is far more prevalent than it actually is.

Out of inexperience or a need to gain professional attention, therapists have been guilty of planting prevailing ideas about child sexual abuse in the minds of vulnerable patients. For example, in a frequently used technique called "guided imagery" the therapist leads the patient through a series of images to bring insight to the patient's emotional problems. More often than not, however, the technique creates in the patient's mind vague images of being helpless and of being overwhelmed by an imposing adult figure. The "discovery" that a parent abused the patient as a child becomes a convenient way to place the blame for his present inadequacies onto anyone but himself.

Most therapists do not deliberately invent abuse scenarios in their patients' minds. Instead, a large factor in the popularity of recovered memory is the therapist's own susceptibility in assuming the truth of prevalent child abuse. In an attempt to be extra sensitive to the very real trauma that child sexual abuse causes, therapists sometimes "may be led to make a hasty diagnosis on the basis of vague symptoms and then probe suggestively for confirming evidence,"[5] according to Elizabeth Loftus.

Putting the Present Above the Past

Therapist Robin Newsome believed strongly in recovered memory until she was struck by her patients' destructive actions after "discovering" their past abuse. Patients accused innocent parents of sexually molesting them as children, which usually caused the disintegration of the family. Newsome found herself questioning how recovered memories of sexual abuse made sense: "I wondered why the Vietnam vet doesn't forget being in Vietnam . . . or the Holocaust survivors [enduring atrocities in Nazi concentration camps]. . . . The problem with real victims of trauma seems just the reverse—they can't forget about those experiences."[6] In light of harm caused by recovered memories and the lack of scientific proof of their validity, Newsome recanted her statements about recovered memories and urged her patients to mend their relationships with their families without relying on possibly invalid memories.

The truth about repressed memories is that they can't be verified through any scientific means. Moreover, they bring considerable pain to both the accuser and the accused. Repressed memories of adults and false allegations made by children both do considerable harm to society. They victimize innocent people, distort an accurate assessment of society's child abuse problem, and waste time and energy that could be used toward healing.

1. Hans Sebald, "Witch-Children: The Myth of the Innocent Child," *Issues in Child Abuse Accusations*, vol. 9, no. 3/4, Summer/Fall 1996, p. 182.

2. Armin A. Brott, "A System Out of Control: The Epidemic of False Allegations of Child Abuse," *Penthouse*, November 1994, www.vix.com/men/falsereport/childabuse/brott94. html.

3. Martin Galloway, "False Abuse Allegations," *Single Dad*, April 29, 1997, www. concernedcounseling.com/ccijournal/mofalseabuse.htm.

4. Elizabeth F. Loftus, "Repressed Memories of Childhood Trauma: Are They Genuine?" *Harvard Mental Health Letter*, March 1993, www.mentalhealth.com/mag1/p5h-mem2. html.

5. Loftus, "Repressed Memories of Childhood Trauma."

6. Quoted in Mark Pendergrast, "First of All, Do No Harm: A Recovered Memory Therapist Recants," *Skeptic*, April 1995, p. 40.

CHAPTER 2

What Causes Child Abuse?

"The changing structure of the average family presents a threat to child safety."

The Breakdown of the Family Causes Child Abuse

The surge in child abuse within the last two decades of the twentieth century is closely tied to the increase in divorce, single-parent households, teenage pregnancy, youth violence, and a general decay of fundamental moral values. The days in which the norm was a loving mom and dad rearing children in a stable household are long gone, along with the basic human truth that children need and deserve emotional, mental, and physical security. The absence of common sense and modern society's deviation from the standards of decency contribute to the plague of child abuse.

What Happened to the Family?

Patrick Fagan, a researcher for the Heritage Foundation, performed a thorough investigation of studies about the child abuse crisis. He found a common theme among them: The changing structure of the average family presents a threat to child safety. "The underlying dynamic of child abuse—the breakdown of marriage and the commitment to love—is spreading like a cancer from poor communities to working-class communities,"[1] comments Fagan.

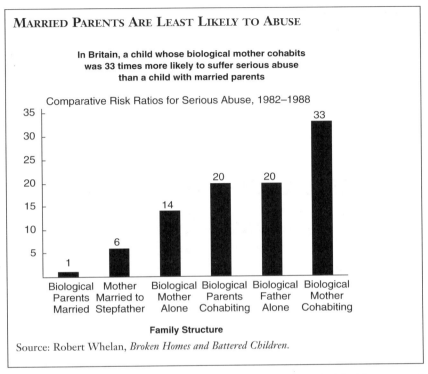

MARRIED PARENTS ARE LEAST LIKELY TO ABUSE

In Britain, a child whose biological mother cohabits
was 33 times more likely to suffer serious abuse
than a child with married parents

Comparative Risk Ratios for Serious Abuse, 1982–1988

Source: Robert Whelan, *Broken Homes and Battered Children.*

The Third National Incidence Study of Child Abuse and
Neglect reveals that abuse and neglect of American children
has increased a staggering 134 percent since 1980. In addition,
the number of children born into unwed or divorced families
more than quadrupled between 1950 and 1990. It is not difficult to determine the strong connection between the disintegration of the family and child abuse. According to the
National Center for Health Statistics, in 1950, 12 out of 100
children were born into unwed or broken families; in 1990,
the proportion had climbed to 58 out of 100 children.

Shifting Priorities Harms Children

Patrick Fagan remarks, "The Family Court Reporter Survey
for England and Wales presents concrete evidence that children are 20 to 33 times safer living with their biological married parents than in other family configurations."[2] This is a
testament to the valuable tradition of a man and woman's

cooperative effort in raising children. But even within two-parent families, priorities seem to have changed drastically. A mother's main concern used to be that of raising her child, especially during the child's first five years, which are considered crucial for healthy mental and emotional development. Now a woman's main concern seems to be her professional status whether or not she has a baby. Not only are parents too often caught up in their careers to pay proper attention to their children, they put these neglected children in extra danger by placing them under the charge of virtual strangers.

One tragic example of the harm resulting from the neglect of career-oriented parents is the case of infant Matthew Eappen. Just a few months after he was born, Matthew was placed under the care of a young nanny while the parents worked long hours at their high-paying jobs. On February 4, 1997, the nanny, Louise Woodward, placed a call to the emergency room to report the infant's mysterious injury. He died five days later and a sensational trial ensued in which Woodward was convicted of killing the baby. Had the infant's mother approached child rearing with the kind of vigor and devotion she seems to have reserved for her career, and nurtured the infant at least through his most vulnerable years, Matthew might still be alive today.

Single Mothers Put Children at Risk

In 1995, over 12 million women headed their households with no husband present, according to the U.S. Census Bureau. Over 13 million children under age eighteen lived in single-mother families. In 1960 the percentage of all births to unmarried mothers was 5 percent; in 1995, it rose to 32 percent. Clearly single-parent households threaten to change the face of the American family. Single-mother families tend to be at lower economic levels than traditional two-parent families; hence, poverty sometimes plays a factor in creating a dangerous situation for the child, who is already in an unstable and potentially violent environment.

Even the presence of a father figure does not eliminate the dangers posed to the child. In fact, a mother's live-in boyfriend or new husband places the child at risk of being sexually abused. "Many studies have shown a relationship between having a stepfather in the home and sexual abuse, especially abuse of daughters,"[3] reports author Karen Kinnear. The incest taboo is strongly reinforced for a child's biological father and by the experience of caring for her since birth, but it may be nonexistent to a male adult who has known the daughter for just a few years or even months. This danger is not limited to America's changing families; it crosses cultural and national lines. Researcher Judith Wallerstein notes that a Canadian study revealed "preschool children in stepfamilies are forty times as likely as children in intact families to suffer physical or sexual abuse."[4]

Children Cannot Raise Children

Another aspect of modern society detrimental to the health of children is the proliferation of teenage pregnancy. Infant homicide was the leading cause of death of babies born in the United States between 1983 and 1991, according to a study conducted by the National Institute of Child Health and Human Development. The study also points out that the most significant contributing factor in infant homicide is teenage motherhood. This seems sadly unsurprising considering that during the 1990s a number of teenage mothers were arrested for giving birth in secrecy and then either killing the newborn or leaving the infant in an isolated area to die. One highly publicized case involved a teenager from Long Island, New York, who gave birth and killed the newborn in a public bathroom during her high school prom. A Canadian case history recounts a sixteen-year-old's attempted murder of her newborn. "She had hidden the pregnancy from her mother and had the baby alone in the bathtub,"[5] reports researcher John Conway.

These teenage abusers are products of a society that has become morally lax. Premarital sex is highly promoted by a culture that functions around the entertainment industry, but education about how to avoid pregnancy during premarital sex is not. Teenage boys old enough to impregnate girls are rarely grown up enough to raise an unexpected child. Teenage mothers are likewise emotionally stunted and can hardly be expected to be competent parents. "Often the parent is so young that he or she has yet to learn the simplest things about child rearing,"[6] explains author Edward Dolan. The tragedy of society's unwillingness to discipline these out-of-control teenagers is the creation of babies that grow up feeling unwanted and forgotten by their parents and society.

Strong Family Values Protect Everyone's Children

Trouble in the family extends to the community. Children in broken families tend to be socially isolated, and thus deprived of a chance to learn positive modes of interacting in a family. Aside from intervening in the lives of troubled nontraditional families, concerned citizens can help alleviate the problem of child abuse by living responsibly. An abused child learns from his environment, guaranteeing a repeat performance of his parent's careless and destructive lifestyle. Personal dedication to strong family values—devotion to the spouse, dedication to raising healthy children, determination to work hard to arrive at family goals—can go a long way in affecting the lives of children.

Until the nation as a whole begins to strengthen the family, which in turn strengthens the community, child abuse will continue to invade more lives. Instead of giving in to the easy lifestyle of divorce, promiscuity, and the pursuit of selfish interests, parents especially must learn the degree of discipline it takes to raise healthy, responsible children and keep a loving family together. A return to basic family values ensures a step in the right direction for children and responsible adults.

1. Patrick F. Fagan, "The Child Abuse Crisis: The Disintegration of Marriage, Family, and the American Community," *Backgrounder*, published by the Heritage Foundation, May 15, 1997, www.heritage.org/library/categories/family/bg1115.html.

2. Fagan, "The Child Abuse Crisis."

3. Karen Kinnear, *Child Sexual Abuse: A Reference Handbook*. Santa Barbara, CA: ABC-CLIO, 1995.

4. Quoted in Barbara Dafoe Whitehead, "Dan Quayle Was Right," *Atlantic Monthly*, April 1993, www.theatlantic.com/atlantic/election/connection/family/danquayl.htm.

5. John F. Conway, "Child Homicide," *Canadian Family in Crisis*, January 25, 1995, www.vix.com/men/battery/studies/child-homicide.html.

6. Edward F. Dolan, *Child Abuse*. New York: Franklin Watts, 1992.

"The truth is that more often than not, a parent's abusive behavior toward her child is not a choice but the result of mental or physical illness that needs to be treated before proper parenting can happen."

Emotionally Unstable Adults Perpetrate Child Abuse

Frequently, child abusers are people with considerable emotional and physical problems. Unfortunately, these unstable adults also have children to look after, impressionable and sometimes completely helpless young people who depend solely on the adult for attention, nurturing, and affection. The tragic result is that, of the 3 million cases of child abuse reported each year, the majority result from dysfunctional relationships between parent and child.

Many conservative critics blame what they perceive as a modern moral vacuum and disintegration of basic values for the way that abusive parents treat their children. This approach implies that parents just need to straighten up and become proper members of society by abiding to traditional modes of child rearing. The truth is that more often than not, a parent's abusive behavior toward her child is not a choice but the result of mental or physical illness that needs to be treated before proper parenting can happen.

Depression Is a Factor
Depression has often been downplayed as an illness but it afflicts many people, regardless of race, gender, religion,

education, or economic level. In his book *The Vulnerable Child*, Richard Weissbourd reveals, "Young children depend heavily on their mothers, and 12 percent of mothers of young children are depressed according to strict diagnostic criteria, and 52 percent report depressive symptoms."[1] Because most infants rely more heavily on their mothers than their fathers, a depressed mother presents considerable dangers to a human being who must constantly be fed, nurtured, even caressed and spoken to affectionately in order to grow and stay healthy.

In addition to emotionally ignoring the child or placing her in physical danger through neglect, a depressed parent can also inflict direct physical abuse on the child. Young and emotionally underdeveloped parents often take out their miseries and frustrations on their helpless children. Richard Weissbourd tells of one parent who "admits that before entering a family support program, when she started to feel helpless and overwhelmed she would hit and scream at her children because 'they were the only things in my life I could control.'" As a result, children who must endure a depressed parent's erratic behavior "may come to feel defeated and deficient,"[2] says Weissbourd.

Depression and feelings of low self-worth are often exacerbated by poverty, which can add to the emotionally fragile parent's stress. A parent already depressed, unable to feel good about herself or her children, and still obliged to worry about paying bills or being able to feed her child can easily be overwhelmed. The person who suffers most from the parent's sense of frustration and helplessness is the innocent child, for whom a parent's influence means everything.

Parental Substance Abuse

Depressed mothers are more likely to smoke, drink, and abuse drugs during pregnancy, according to Richard Weissbourd, resulting in health problems for the infant. With or without depression as a factor, studies indicate that a

Alcohol and drug abuse often lead to depression, fits of violent rage, and impaired judgment, all of which can increase the risk of child abuse.

major contributing factor to child abuse is alcohol or drug addiction. According to the Children of Alcoholics Foundation, 40 percent of confirmed child abuse cases involve the use of alcohol or other drugs. "Children of alcoholics suffer more injuries and poisonings than children in the general population. Alcohol and other substances may act as disinhibitors, lessening impulse control and allowing parents to behave abusively,"[3] reports child advocacy group Prevent Child Abuse America. In other words, nearly half a million children are abused or neglected by a parent with alcohol or drug problems.

A volatile environment populated by drug dealers and other adult strangers can present considerable physical dangers to the neglected child. But even if a child's environment is limited to immediate family members, a parent's alcohol or drug habit alone is a dangerous factor in child abuse and neglect. Children neglected by alcohol- or drug-abusing parents do not receive the very necessary emotional nurturing or mental development; instead, they sometimes receive physical abuse. Neglected children often try to gain their parents' attention through various kinds of behavior, often very typical of developing children. Unfortunately, the child's call for attention can often provoke anger in the drug-influenced parent. Anger often leads to violence directed against the child or another family member.

Domestic Violence Has a Great Impact

One adult's abuse of another adult in the household is usually referred to as domestic violence. Violent husbands are frequent culprits, battering their wives, sometimes in front of their children. Other times, a stepfather or the mother's live-in boyfriend may develop a pattern of physically abusing the mother. The American Humane Association notes a strong connection between domestic violence and child abuse: "Child abuse is 15 times more likely to occur in households where adult domestic violence is also present."[4] Perhaps a child gets in the way during a fight between parents. Or a child may attempt to intervene, taking the blows a father or other male adult intends for the child's mother.

Disturbingly, many battered women are also child abusers. "The severity of child abuse, and the manner in which children are abused, bears a strong resemblance to the type of maltreatment experienced by their mothers,"[5] explains the American Humane Association. Battered women are often so incapacitated by their own abuse that they are unable to give proper care to their children. Sometimes the tremendous stress of living in constant peril causes women to take out their anxieties on their children. They may beat and berate their children in a misguided attempt to turn them into "perfect angels" who could not possibly provoke the anger of the batterer.

A Cycle of Abuse Persists

In addition to the direct damage of abuse, children suffer greatly from witnessing abuse on a regular basis. They begin to view hitting and the devaluing of individuals as the norm and carry this negative attitude into adulthood. "Parents who were abused children are six times more likely to abuse their own children than are parents from 'normal' homes,"[6] reports journalist Elaine Landau, who specializes in youth issues. Because the parents did not receive genuine love and consideration from their own parents, they may simply be ignorant of their children's needs. Hence, this pattern of abuse is passed down from generation to generation.

Neglect and physical abuse are some of the common forms of maltreatment children suffer at the hands of unstable parents. However, sexual abuse is also a tragic reality for those who perpetuate the cycle of abuse. Gail Ryan, director of the Perpetration Prevention Project, explains, "Many sexual abusers experienced victimization themselves as children (physical, sexual, and/or emotional). For those perpetrators who were sexually abused, early offenses sometimes appear to be reenactments of their own victimization."[7]

To put a stop to the continuing abuse of children, many of whom are born into patterns of violence and are therefore at an immediate disadvantage, society must give those families the very necessary attention they need. Indeed, in some cases the life of a child is jeopardized for as long as an unstable parent's potential danger to his or her child is ignored. The signs of unstable parenting are not so difficult to recognize. They include parents who are depressed or detached from the world and children who seem to try too hard to compensate for their parents' unpredictable behavior. Poverty, which is not difficult to detect, often acts as a warning sign that children are not receiving the proper care they need. And erratic behavior due to alcohol or drug use must always be confronted when children are concerned. By educating the public and creating intervention programs to place children in more positive settings, society can take steps toward giving innocent kids a chance to be "normal."

1. Richard Weissbourd, *The Vulnerable Child: What Really Hurts America's Children and What We Can Do About It.* Reading, MA: Addison Wesley Longman, 1996, p. 73.

2. Weissbourd, *The Vulnerable Child*, p. 73.

3. Prevent Child Abuse America, "The Relationship Between Parental Alcohol or Other Drug Problems and Child Maltreatment," September 1996, www.childabuse.org/fs14.html.

4. American Humane Association, "The Link Between Child Abuse and Domestic Abuse," *Child Protection Leader,* September 1994, www.yesican.org/articles/linkadv.html.

5. American Humane Association, "The Link Between Child Abuse and Domestic Abuse."

6. Elaine Landau, *Child Abuse: An American Epidemic.* Englewood Cliffs, NJ: Silver Burdett, 1990, p. 25.

7. Gail Ryan, "The Sexual Abuser," in Mary Edna Helfer, Ruth S. Kempe, and Richard D. Krugman, eds., *The Battered Child.* Chicago: University of Chicago Press, 1997, p. 330.

"What began as a desire to discipline the child can get out of control and escalate into infliction of physical pain that simply must be identified as child abuse."

Corporal Punishment Leads to Child Abuse

In some Scandinavian countries, corporal punishment is outlawed. This means that it is illegal for any adult authority figure—a parent or teacher, for example—to spank or hit a child, even if the intent is to discipline. Unfortunately, this is not the case in the United States. In North America, some teachers are allowed to use corporal punishment in school and parents are usually given the freedom to use corporal punishment at their own discretion. Many consider spanking to be an acceptable and necessary means of disciplining a child. As a result of lenient social attitudes toward corporal punishment and the misguided use of it by frustrated parents, children endure considerable abuse, which can sometimes be fatal.

The term *corporal punishment* has serious connotations, implying a disciplinary tool or drastic measure reserved for special circumstances. However, some parents make regular use of corporal punishment in daily interactions with their children. "For some parents spanking means hitting the child on the buttocks. For others it refers to all hitting of a child, such as slapping the hand or the child's face. Spanking, hitting, and slapping are all forms of physical punishment or corporal punishment,"[1] states Laurel Swanson, editor of *Positive*

Parenting magazine. Calling the physical act "spanking" instead of "corporal punishment" may help alleviate the guilt some parents feel from performing an action without any real consideration of its long-term impact on the child.

Why Do Parents Spank Their Children?

Parents spank their children because society accepts the practice as justifiable behavior for adults. In a 1994 *USA Today*/CNN Gallup Poll, 67 percent of a national sample of American adults agreed with the statement, "It is sometimes necessary to discipline a child with a good hard spanking."[2] According to authors Murray Straus and Carrie Yodanis, "More than 90 percent of American parents use corporal punishment on toddlers, and more than half continue this into the early teen years."[3] Statistics vary, but all surveys indicate that parents still view corporal punishment as part of the job of raising children.

In their study of physical discipline and abuse, Ellen Whipple and Cheryl Richey found that, despite a growing social movement away from the use of physical force against children, many American parents use corporal punishment in varying degrees. "Like alcohol consumption, that continues to be socially and legally permissible when used moderately and within certain boundaries, physical discipline of young children appears to be found permissible by many 'normal,' nonabusive American parents if utilized within the context of competent parenting."[4] As long as a parent acts like a normal, respectable member of the community, onlookers will rarely question his mode of "disciplining" his child.

Parents often justify their use of spanking as a way of teaching their children right from wrong. However, the truth is that corporal punishment is more an expression of a parent's own frustrations and personal sense of inadequacy than an effective way to instill socially acceptable behavior in the child. Unfortunately, the child's physical and mental vulnerability causes him to accept the parent's punishment, which may be interpreted by the parent as learning and maturing.

But physical punishment hardly contributes to a child's growth. Studies have indicated that corporal punishment does very little in teaching a child to be cooperative or to make constructive decisions in society. In that light, corporal punishment is clearly nothing more than abuse.

"Disciplining" Can Harm

Parents often draw distinctions between different degrees of physical abuse, considering some behaviors more or less harmless and others as "crossing the line" into abuse. But most forms of physical contact carry the possibility of harming the child. Jan Hunt of the Natural Child Project warns, "Even relatively moderate spanking can be physically dangerous. Blows to the lower end of the spinal column send shock waves along the length of the spine, and may injure the child."[5] There is no guarantee that the parent will know the precise amount of physical contact to use to avoid permanent damage.

In fact, there is no guarantee that the physically aggressive parent can maintain control over her own emotions or remain rational in heated moments when undisciplined children are confronted. End Physical Punishment of Children, a child advocacy group, describes how a possibly well-intentioned attempt to discipline an unruly child can escalate into something entirely different:

> When a parent spanks, it means that he/she does not deal with the behavior in a way that would lead to a more permanent change. Spanking seems to lose effectiveness over time and parents have to hit harder and harder raising the danger of physical injury; of the almost three million child abuse reports made annually in the early 1990's, about 30 percent involved physical punishment.[6]

What began as a desire to discipline the child can get out of control and escalate into infliction of physical pain that simply must be identified as child abuse.

Corporal Punishment Is Not Educational

Corporal punishment leads to child abuse in another way—through its perpetuation of aggressive reactions to conflict. Children who endure corporal punishment, rather than becoming upstanding members of society, go on to exhibit aggressive behavior. *The Harvard Mental Health Letter* notes that in a study of abused children, those who were in turn aggressive in the classroom "misinterpreted social situations, attributed hostile intentions to others, viewed aggression as a good way to gain their ends, and failed to generate sensible solutions to everyday problems."[7] As adults, the victims of corporal punishment usually become violent themselves, venting their frustrations with life's everyday problems on their own children. Thus another child is abused, this time by a former abused child, and the cycle of child abuse continues.

In schools, the use of corporal punishment at the discretion of teachers carries high risks. The National Coalition to Abolish Corporal Punishment in Schools reports, "Injuries occur. Bruises are common. Broken bones are not unusual. Children's deaths have occurred in the U.S. due to school corporal punishment."[8] Only twenty-seven states ban the use of corporal punishment in the schools. The U.S. Department of Education reports that in the 1993–1994 school year, nearly five hundred thousand students were subjected to corporal punishment. Arkansas (13.4 percent), Mississippi (10.9 percent), and Alabama (7.3 percent) were the states with the highest incidence of physical punishment of students by educators, according to the U.S. Department of Education. As long as corporal punishment is allowed in some schools and not banned across the entire nation, there will be children who learn that physical punishment is acceptable.

Spanking Should Be Outlawed

The general public's widespread acceptance of corporal punishment undermines the very serious nature of the practice. Instead of pretending there is no real harm in swatting a child's bottom, society should look for effective alternatives in influencing a child's development. In 1979, Sweden banned the use of corporal punishment, a measure that has been effective in encouraging more positive modes of parenting. In the two decades following the ban, support for the use of corporal punishment in Sweden fell from over half the population to just under a third.

Researcher Ake W. Edfeldt says that in today's Swedish society, "Nobody can stand up anymore and publicly state that, 'I am a good father. I use corporal punishment because I think it is needed.' It is the other way around now. Today such a person is looked upon as a bad father."[9] In addition, rates of child abuse have lowered since Sweden's banning of corporal punishment. According to researcher Joan Durrant, "By the mid-1980s, Swedish rates of physical discipline and child abuse were half those found in the U.S., and the Swedish rate of child death due to abuse was less than one-third the American rate."[10]

Such a positive stance against the still-accepted family practice of spanking is clearly effective and should be adopted by more societies in the interest of protecting children. Given the troubling number of children whose parents abuse them under the guise of discipline, the use of corporal punishment by parents should be outlawed by the government or at least frowned upon by responsible parents. Children deserve to be taught the valuable skills of solving problems constructively without resorting to physical violence. In the long run, encouraging nonviolent parenting will be most effective in reducing the problem of child abuse.

1. Laurel Swanson, "What the Research Says About Physical Punishment," *Positive Parenting*, December 1, 1998, www.extension.umn.edu/Documents/D/E/Other/6961_01.html.

2. Quoted in Swanson, "What the Research Says About Physical Punishment."

3. Murray A. Straus and Carrie L. Yodanis, "Corporal Punishment of Children and

Depression and Suicide in Adulthood," in Joan McCord, ed., *Coercion and Punishment in Long-Term Perspective*. New York: Cambridge University Press, 1994, p. 62.

4. Ellen E. Whipple and Cheryl A. Richey, "Crossing the Line from Physical Discipline to Child Abuse: How Much Is Too Much?" *Child Abuse & Neglect*, May 1997, p. 441.

5. Jan Hunt, "Ten Reasons Not to Hit Your Kids," 1996, www.naturalchild.com/jan_hunt/tenreasons.html.

6. End Physical Punishment of Children, "Spanking: Facts & Fiction," February 3, 1999, www.stophitting.com/spanking.htm.

7. Kenneth A. Dodge, John E. Bates, and Gregory S. Pettit, "How the Cycle of Abuse Works," *Harvard Mental Health Letter*, May 1991, www.mentalhealth.com/mag1/p5h-abu3.html.

8. National Coalition to Abolish Corporal Punishment in Schools, "Arguments Against Corporal Punishment," *Facts About Corporal Punishment*, October 20, 1998, www.stophitting.com/facts_about_corporal_punishment.htm.

9. Ake W. Edfeldt, "The Swedish 1979 Aga Ban Plus Fifteen," *Family Violence Against Children: A Challenge for Society*. New York: Walter de Gruyter, 1996, p. 35.

10. Joan E. Durrant, "The Swedish Ban on Corporal Punishment: Its History and Effects," *Family Violence Against Children*, Detlev Fresee, Wiebke Horn, and Kai-D. Bussman, eds. p. 22.

CHAPTER 3

How Can Child Abuse Be Reduced?

"A rigorous and cooperative system of children's protective services, law enforcement, legal and medical professionals, and every responsible citizen of adult age should work together to reduce child abuse."

A More Aggressive Child Protection System Would Reduce Child Abuse

The alarmingly high number of child abuse cases reported each year indicates the need for a more effective system of child protection to combat this worsening problem. A rigorous and cooperative system of children's protective services, law enforcement, legal and medical professionals, and every responsible citizen of adult age should work together to reduce child abuse. Their common goal should be to establish a solid system of child protection that takes real action toward preventing child abuse and healing social ills.

The term *child protective services* (CPS) refers to state agencies charged with protecting children from abuse and neglect. Each state receives federal funds to establish programs and organizations that combat child abuse at the local level. The National Center on Child Abuse and Neglect explains that state CPS agencies are responsible for collecting reports of child abuse and neglect, investigating the charges, assessing whether child abuse is a factor, providing psychological or legal counseling as needed, and developing court reports. The responsibilities of CPS social workers are sometimes shared with law enforcement and the state courts. Unfortunately, not all of these responsibilities are fulfilled adequately. As a consequence, children who need protection suffer greatly.

Stronger CPS intervention could eliminate senseless, shameful tragedies that appear frequently in the pages of newspapers around the world. For example, in Durango, Colorado, Lawrence Gierisch kidnapped his seven-year-old daughter Gianni Barrows in January 1999 for the second time, then murdered her and committed suicide. Tragically, after the first time the daughter was kidnapped, her mother, Lori Barrow, had begged the courts to prevent Gierisch's unsupervised visitation with Gianni, but the courts denied the mother's request. If the courts had been more concerned with the child's safety than with the father's visitation rights, or if investigations into the case had been more thorough, this tragedy would have been avoided.

The System Does Not Do Enough

Sociologist Karl Zinsmeister laments, "Our standards of child protection have fallen to scandalously low levels. . . . Many child-protection agencies are now doing little more than preventing murder and sometimes they fail even to do that."[1] The tragedies abound because of a lack of aggressive action on the part of CPS agencies. The courts are often reluctant to remove children from parental custody unless there is clear indication that the child is in immediate physical danger, which can irreparably harm the child.

Zinsmeister describes the tragic incident of Michaela Robinson, an infant born addicted to cocaine. Even though the mother was very uncooperative with child protective services and the child showed signs of neglect, social workers did not feel justified in separating the child from its mother. As a result, Michaela was found at age six months emaciated in an infant seat. According to authorities, cocaine poisoning was the cause of death; crack smoke blown into the baby's face and mouth in an attempt to pacify her was possibly the source of the fatal intoxication. "In instances where parents prove unwilling or unable to provide their children with the care and oversight they need, our child-protection services must have the resources and will to act,"[2] says Zinsmeister. Unfortunately, they don't.

Unfortunate Consequences of Budget Cuts

The lack of vigor in state CPS agencies stems in part from recent budget cuts. New York City, for example, "had to pass on severe funding cuts to voluntary agencies that contract with the city to provide preventive and foster care services to vulnerable children and families,"[3] according to the Citizens

With limited goverment funding, social service workers do their best to investigate reports of suspected child abuse.

Committee for Children. Inadequate funding from state and federal governments means less money to employ qualified workers or train employees in the specific tasks of investigating and assessing child abuse cases.

Says *New York Times* columnist Bob Herbert, "Even as the money was being cut, the number of reports of abused and neglected children was increasing, which meant, inevitably, that child protective caseloads would increase. This is how children get killed."[4] This lack of state funding reveals what a low priority the government places on protecting the nation's children. It also points to the average citizen's unwillingness to force his or her government to allocate more tax money to CPS agencies, which desperately need the money to perform competently.

Vicki Ashton's study on novice CPS workers found that the inexperienced caseworkers are not fully aware of all their responsibilities as "mandated reporters" (government employees with the authority to determine child abuse situations). Ashton notes that "unless a parent's behavior is blatantly abusive, workers are not likely to report the incident."[5]   Clearly, caseworkers need more training and lighter caseloads to make them more diligent investigators, especially in situations where children are being abused by a parent. Family dynamics often maintain secrecy, resisting effective investigation by caseworkers. But if the system of laws is to favor the suffering child over the adult perpetrator, child welfare workers need the cooperative efforts of other agencies.

Working with Various Agencies

An aggressive system of child protection entails the quick action of CPS caseworkers but also requires that other local government agencies, such as law enforcement and medical professionals, assume active roles in child protection. For example, law enforcement is sometimes responsible for investigating reports of child abuse but usually only after CPS caseworkers have already made their assessment. A more effective strategy would be to involve law enforcement at the same time as CPS caseworkers to establish different perspectives on potential child abuse. As Michael Weber, associate director of the National Committee to Prevent Child Abuse, suggests, law enforcement's involvement would "assure that the criminal aspect of suspected maltreatment is thoroughly investigated and that the evidence necessary for criminal prosecution is adequately safeguarded."[6] Thus, cooperative effort between agencies creates an efficient system in which few details are overlooked.

Legal and judicial system professionals also play a role in child protection, contributing to a weak system or strong system, depending on their level of individual activity and cooperation with other agencies. "Assuming we all agree that in our democratic society every child has a right to receive at least minimally adequate care, we must have legal means of ascertaining the level of each child's safety,"[7] says legal counsel Donald Bross. An aggressive legal system would effectively prepare CPS caseworkers, expert witnesses, and the child victim to testify in court and assure that legal actions are taken to benefit the child. Attorneys representing victims of child abuse must work with other agencies to prosecute the abusers and win legal redress. In its guide to effective investigation of child abuse cases, the Office of Juvenile Justice and Delinquency Prevention notes that "an investigator's failure to collect [relevant] information leaves the prosecutor without one of the most important pieces of corroborative evidence for proving an intentional act of child abuse."[8]

Educators and medical professionals also must play active roles in the system of child protection. Educators are frequently the people in closest contact with children outside of their families. They are in a good position to notice signs of child abuse and neglect, which emphasizes their responsibilities to report abuse and keep CPS caseworkers informed of changes in children's conditions. Although not usually authorized to receive reports of child abuse, medical professionals are responsible for identifying and reporting suspected cases of child abuse and neglect.

Everyone Plays a Part

Even ordinary citizens have responsibilities in the community's interest in protecting children. In Nevada, this became apparent when seven-year-old Sherrice Iverson was molested and strangled in a Las Vegas casino by nineteen-year-old Jeremy Strohmeyer. According to the *Los Angeles Times*, Strohmeyer's friend David Cash "witnessed the beginning of the assault but did not intervene or report it to the police."[9] Under a bill signed on June 11, 1999, two years after Sherrice's death, adults are required to notify police if they witness child abuse. If they fail to do so, they could be sentenced to six months in jail. This is reasonable: Shirking the responsibility of intervening for a helpless child should be considered criminal.

CPS caseworkers, law enforcement, legal professionals, medical professionals, teachers, and even neighbors should all work together to effectively prevent child abuse. Teamwork, a rigorous attitude, and dedication to child safety will ensure a stronger system of child protection. "By establishing a child protection agency with the capacity to offer more than one response and to work in collaboration with other community agencies, this emerging policy trend has the promise of enabling each community to respond differentially with the greatest likelihood of protecting each child from future abuse or neglect,"[10] says Michael Weber. In the end, strengthening the system of child protective services serves the interests of every member of society.

1. Karl Zinsmeister, "Growing Up Scared," *Atlantic Monthly*, June 1990, p. 55.

2. Zinsmeister, "Growing Up Scared."

3. Quoted in Bob Herbert, "An Unending Tragedy," *New York Times*, February 26, 1998.

4. Herbert, "An Unending Tragedy."

5. Vicki Ashton, "Worker Judgments of Seriousness About and Reporting of Suspected Child Maltreatment," *Child Abuse & Neglect*, June 1999, p. 546.

6. Michael W. Weber, "The Assessment of Child Abuse: A Primary Function of Child Protective Services," Mary Edna Helfer, Ruth S. Kempe, and Richard D. Krugman, eds., *The Battered Child*. Chicago: University of Chicago Press, 1997, p. 129.

7. Donald C. Bross, "The Legal Context of Child Abuse and Neglect: Balancing the Rights of Children and Parents in a Democratic Society," Helfer, Kempe, and Krugman, eds., *The Battered Child*, p. 62.

8. Office of Juvenile Justice and Delinquency Prevention, *Battered Child Syndrome: Investigating Physical Abuse and Homicide*. Washington, DC: Office of Juvenile Justice and Delinquency Prevention, 1996.

9. "Nevada OKs Penalty for Witnesses Who Don't Report Child Abuse," *Los Angeles Times*, June 12, 1999.

10. Weber, "The Assessment of Child Abuse," p. 148.

*"Child protective services' unchecked authority has con-
tributed to tragedies that could have been avoided with
common sense and consideration of individual lives."*

A More Aggressive Child Protection System Would Harm Children and Families

Adults who are too lazy to do their part as responsible members of society will let others take over and make decisions
about their lives. Such is the case in the troubling issue of
child abuse. The dangerously overzealous child protection
system has been given so much power and authority to intervene in families that instead of effecting positive changes for
victimized children, it is ruining the lives of innocent adults
and many of the children it seeks to protect.

The Mondale Act of 1973 established a system of child
abuse detection, prosecution, and prevention programs to
handle reported cases of abuse. The child protection system
consists mainly of government-funded and state-established
child protective services (CPS) in every state. Each state's CPS
agency has the power to investigate potential cases of child
abuse, substantiate a reported case of abuse, and involve other
local government agencies such as law enforcement and legal
professionals to protect children and prosecute suspected

abusers. Although the child protection system involves the police and criminal prosecutors, it is for the most part managed by CPS caseworkers, who have gotten carried away with their power and authority.

Overzealous and Undertrained

As one way of assuring that their interests and power are maintained, child protective services often exaggerate the occurrence of child abuse. By promoting the idea that child abuse is rampant in society, the child protection system retains its necessary status. "By portraying horror stories of brutally abused children as the norm, America's 'child savers' (a term they gave themselves in the 19th Century) have persuaded us to cede to them unprecedented power over the lives of children,"[1] explains the National Coalition for Child Protection Reform (NCCPR). Because the federal government considers the business of protecting children a community problem to be handled by local government, state CPS agencies are given ultimate power to decide what constitutes child abuse and how victims' lives will be altered.

The unfortunate fact is that although CPS caseworkers are given considerable authority over people's lives, they are not adequately trained to make such big decisions. For example, former CPS caseworker Paula Garcia notes that her training consisted of reading a few policy manuals and relying on the experience of the "seasoned" caseworkers around her. Says Garcia, "I knew very early on I would not learn much from my 'seasoned' co-workers. They had very poor skills."[2] Researcher Rick Thoma believes this inadequate training is common in most states. "In New York City, caseworkers receive only twenty days of training, most of which focuses not on child development but on filling out forms and other paperwork tasks,"[3] comments Thoma.

The educational requirements for CPS workers vary from state to state, but the American Public Welfare Association indicates that at least ten states do not require a college degree and fewer than twenty-five states train their workers before they take on actual cases. NCCPR fears that society has "given untrained, inexperienced, sometimes incompetent workers the power to enter our homes, interrogate and strip-search our children and even remove them to foster care entirely on their own authority."[4] This fear is substantiated by numerous cases in which children are torn from their families on scant evidence of child abuse.

Overstepping Its Function

The child protection system pursues overzealous interventions and careless investigations. When CPS agencies suspect child abuse, they have the power to remove the child from the allegedly harmful environment. Unfortunately, CPS caseworkers often remove children from their homes because this is an easier safety measure than a thorough and time-consuming investigation of the situation. According to NCCPR, there are too many tragic incidents of children having been removed from their homes in the interest of "erring on the side of the child;" that is, there has been no determination that the child's parents have actually abused the child. For example, after receiving reports of possible neglect, CPS caseworkers placed nine-year-old Angela Bennett in a foster home even though a therapist later described her parents as "excellent." In the foster home, Angela was beaten and raped by another foster child.

Child protective services did not believe Angela's claim of assault in her foster home, even though she had bruises all over her body, and even after a medical examination showed she had been raped. As a way of denying responsibility for their thoughtless displacement of Angela, her CPS caseworker accused the nine-year-old of being seductive and soliciting sex. "The act of removing a child from everything loving and familiar and placing him or her with strangers is an act of brutality in itself. That brutality is compounded when children are moved over and over again,"[5] says NCCPR.

Such egregious errors are common in a system whose representatives are free of oversight and accountability. In their online book *In Pursuit of Justice*, Steven and Ellie Lee describe how their entire family was victimized by a system designed to protect children and help families: "When a government agency undertakes the cause of protecting children from harm and gives individuals the authority to make judgments about situations in which they may have neither the wisdom nor the experience to interpret correctly, mistakes can occur."[6]

The System Benefits from Mistakes

Angela and the Lees were casualties of a system that seeks monetary profit over the well-being of individual children. Social commentator Bob Kirkpatrick reports that states "make a profit whenever they take a child as their ward."[7] The federal government pays almost twenty thousand dollars annually for each child in foster care. Fifty-five hundred of that goes toward the child's basic needs and another seven thousand is paid to case administrators. The state keeps the rest: In the end, the state makes a profit of nearly eight thousand dollars for each child who is placed in foster care.

While government agencies profit from their mistakes, innocent parents can be financially ruined by them. According to Bob Kirkpatrick, the most harmful effects of a child protection system propelled by profit are that "families get divided, parents are driven into financial ruin trying to prove their innocence, and all of those involved—the children too—are subjected to such emotional trauma that their lives are permanently and negatively altered."[8] The financial burden alone places most families at the mercy of government agencies. Texans Against False Allegations estimates that legal fees to fight an accusation of child abuse average ten thousand dollars. But other costs include another eight thousand dollars to retrieve a child placed in state-run foster care and over thirty thousand dollars for government-mandated family counseling.

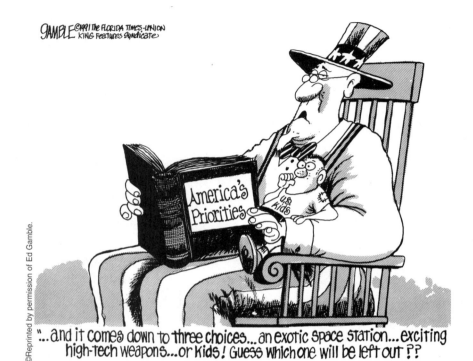

GAMBLE ©1991 THE FLORIDA TIMES-UNION
KING FEATURES SYNDICATE

©Reprinted by permission of Ed Gamble.

"...and it comes down to three choices...an exotic space station...exciting high-tech weapons...or kids! Guess which one will be left out ??"

A System Out of Control

The child protection system's undeserved authority has hurt many innocent people. For instance, a sweeping investigation of an alleged child sex ring in Wenatchee, Washington, resulted in criminal charges against over forty CPS professionals who "pursued convictions with a damaging zeal," report Andrew Schneider and Mike Barber. The CPS workers apparently coerced false accusations from terrified children, many of whom later recanted their statements. According to Schneider and Barber, years after the Wenatchee fiasco, many of those victimized children were still separated from their families. "Numerous children say they were hurt horribly— not by rapists but by state . . . caseworkers and counselors and therapists hired by [the state's] Office of Child Protective Services,"[9] explain Schneider and Barber.

It is clear that child protective services have overstepped their bounds. They have interfered in situations where "help" has been neither wanted nor needed. They have torn apart families and ruined the lives of innocent children. They have branded conscientious adults as criminals and stripped them of their parental rights. Dr. Richard Gardner, a clinical professor of child psychiatry, explains that many false allegations of child abuse emerge from "a complex network of social workers, mental health professionals, and law enforcement officials that actually encourages charges of child abuse— whether they're reasonable or not."[10] All the while, the real problem of child abuse remains. It persists because the child protection system is too busy wielding its power over the lives of respectable citizens instead of concentrating on better training of their workers and developing new methods of investigating and treating child abuse.

Child abuse cannot be reduced by giving child protective services more power than they already have. If anything, this system is too powerful and too eager to intrude in the lives of innocent people. Child protective services' unchecked authority has contributed to tragedies that could have been avoided with common sense and consideration of individual lives. In order for child abuse to be reduced, child protective services should be reevaluated and their methods changed to focus attention on the real victims out there, instead of creating new ones.

1. National Coalition for Child Protection Reform, "Introduction: How the War Against Child Abuse Became a War Against Children," *Issues,* 1997, www.nccpr.org/issues/1.html.

2. Quoted in Rick Thoma, "A Critical Look at the Child Welfare System: Caseworker Training," *Lifting the Veil,* June 27, 1998, http://home.rica.net/rthoma/training.htm.

3. Thoma, "A Critical Look at the Child Welfare System."

4. National Coalition for Child Protection Reform, "Introduction."

5. National Coalition for Child Protection Reform, "They 'Erred on the Side of the Child'— Some Case Histories," *Issues,* 1997, www.nccpr.org/issues/2.html.

6. Steven and Ellie Lee, *In Pursuit of Justice,* 1994, www.efn.org/~srl/justice.html.

7. Bob Kirkpatrick, "Recent Escalation in Child Abuse Charges Tied to Divorce," *The Men's Issues Page*, March 15, 1995, www.vix.com/pub/men/falsereport/commentary/ass-law-judge.html.

8. Kirkpatrick, "Recent Escalation in Child Abuse Charges Tied to Divorce."

9. Andrew Schneider and Mike Barber, "Children Hurt by the System," *Seattle Post-Intelligencer*, February 24, 1998, http://www.seattle-pi.com/pi/powertoharm/therapy.html.

10. Quoted in Armin A. Brott, "A System Out of Control: The Epidemic of False Allegations of Child Abuse," *Penthouse*, November 1994, www.vix.com/men/falsereport/child-abuse/brott94.html.

"If only one child is saved from abuse because of a community notification law, then the law has been successful."

Community Notification Laws Help Prevent Child Abuse

What appeared to be a pleasant summer day in 1994 turned into a gruesome tragedy in many lives. That day, Jesse Timmendequas raped seven-year-old Megan Kanka, strangled her, put a plastic bag over her head, and dumped her body in a nearby park. Then Timmendequas casually joined Megan's parents and neighbors in their search for the missing girl. Only after Timmendequas was arrested did Megan's parents learn that the neighbor across the street was a twice-convicted sex offender on parole. Obviously, this information came too late for Megan's parents.

Megan Kanka's senseless death prompted a nationwide movement to take action to prevent similar tragedies. A key aspect of Megan's case was that her murder might have been prevented if her parents had known their neighbor was a repeat child sexual abuser. Given that many child sexual abusers repeat their crimes and harm more than one child in their lives, targeting repeat offenders is a logical step in preventing further child abuse. In New Jersey, where Megan was murdered, a sex offender registration and community notification law went into effect as "Megan's Law." Megan's Law requires repeat sex offenders to register personal information with the local police whenever they move and allows states to notify communities when sex offenders are released.

Megan's Law has served as a model for other states that have established their own community notification laws. According to the Center for Sex Offender Management, "As a result of increased public concern about predatory sex offenders and federal financial incentives, all 50 states have now passed sex offender registration laws, and 47 states have included community notification components."[1] This movement has made the general public more aware of the dangers that children face on a daily basis. The point of the laws is not, as some critics claim, to create a police state in which every adult's background is scrutinized, but rather to give parents the information they need to thwart potential tragedies. If only one child is saved from abuse because of a community notification law, then the law has been successful.

Prevention Reduces Child Abuse

Community notification laws do work to prevent child abuse and are absolutely necessary as protective measures by concerned citizens. They make for safer communities. Megan's Law, for example, went into effect in California on September 26, 1996. Law enforcement agencies distributed notification flyers to various businesses and residential districts with the name, photograph, convictions, and parole conditions of sex offenders residing nearby. Since that time, a large number of offender identifications have allowed parents to protect their children from potential abuse. In one instance, a mom recognized a man involved with the local Little League as being a "high risk" sex offender and notified local authorities. An investigation resulted in the sex offender's arrest for molesting eight teenage boys.

In another example, a fourteen-year-old girl was walking home from school when a man in a car attempted to lure her to the car under the guise of asking for directions. The girl refused because she recognized him from one of the community notification flyers and instead left to contact the police. As a result, the suspect was arrested because he violated his parole for attempting sexual contact with a minor. "These actions may have helped prevent future offenses as they either removed the known offender from a situation where others are vulnerable, or provided potential victims with information they could use to protect themselves and others,"[2] states former California attorney general Dan Lungren.

Many parents do not report incidents of child sexual abuse in part because the task of pursuing criminal charges against a child molester is stressful and intrusive. "Even though they are outraged, shame and the fear of subjecting their child to the trauma of a court trial deters them from seeking justice,"[3] explains legislator Tere Renteria. Thus, community notification laws offer a preemptive strategy for confronting child molesters before any harm is done to children and before the stress of after-the-fact prosecution.

Protection Above Privacy

Critics of community notification laws complain that offenders who have served their sentences are punished again by being robbed of their privacy. However, given the irreparable harm done to a child if a child abuser strikes again, it seems fitting that the offender should suffer the irreversible consequences of his terrible act. Linda Meilink, the managing editor of a small California newspaper, fired her own staff writer after she discovered he had a record of two convictions for sexual offenses against children. She also decided to notify her community by printing his name in the newspaper. Meilink feels strongly that she did the right thing: "Which is more important: the right of a child to grow up unmolested or of a man to live in peace? By printing those names, are we ruining the life of someone who has been rehabilitated and served his time? I don't know, but if

I'm going to err, I'm going to err on the side of innocent children in the community."[4]

Child molesters should not be easily forgiven even for a single offense. During that one incident, an innocent child has suffered such terrible trauma that it permanently impairs that child's emotional and physical well-being. "Megan's Law statutes, which require paroled sex offenders to register with authorities, are first and foremost about acknowledging the devastating effects that sexual assault has on victims and their families and protecting communities, to the extent possible, from being victimized by sex offenders,"[5] explains Adriana Ramelli, director of the Sex Abuse Treatment Center in Honolulu, Hawaii. Maintaining safe neighborhoods for children is crucial for a healthy society. If deviant adults are not set apart from responsible people trying to live normal lives, the sickness threatens to inflict the whole of society. Child molesters—even so-called rehabilitated offenders—do not deserve to have their needs for privacy placed above children's absolute need for safety. They should expect that after they've committed a heinous act, they will never be able to wash their hands of their crime. At least this would be an ounce of compensation for children who are permanently marked with shame.

Strengthening the Community

The National Victim Center supports the use of community notification laws as a means of supporting every responsible person's efforts toward education and awareness, two modes of reducing child abuse. "If the public is provided adequate notice and information about sexually violent predators and certain other offenders, the community can develop constructive plans to prepare themselves and their children for the offender's release,"[6] says a center spokesperson. Communities can then work with local law enforcement to gather information about community rights and responsibilities and educate parents and children.

Additionally, to maintain their effectiveness, laws must not be allowed to become obsolete or inadequate but continue to meet changing cultural contexts. In New York, for example, Governor George Pataki created the "Megan's Law Task Force" to build on the services of Megan's Law. The task force explored ways to make Megan's Law even stronger and more effective, and called on the testimonies of experts, victims, and concerned citizens' groups.

Community notification laws are effective and can be made more effective with conscientious application and monitoring by parents and other adults who value child security. Given that 25 percent of girls and 17 percent of boys are sexually assaulted before they turn eighteen, community notification laws are crucial tools in helping parents protect their children from such crimes. Even if the number of child sexual abuse cases is reduced because of community notification laws, the laws should be constantly revitalized and vigilantly enforced.

1. Quoted in Anthony J. Petrosino and Carolyn Petrosino, "The Public Safety Potential of Megan's Law in Massachusetts: An Assessment from a Sample of Criminal Sexual Psychopaths," *Crime & Delinquency*, January 1999, p. 141.

2. Dan Lungren, "Results: Safe Communities," *Megan's Law Report*, May 1998, http://caag.state.ca.us/megan/meganrpt.htm.

3. Tere Renteria, "Keep Sex Offenders Away from Children," *San Diego Union-Tribune*, July 17, 1997.

4. Quoted in Judith Sheppard, "Double Punishment?" *American Journalism Review*, November 1997, http://ajr.newslink.org.

5. Adriana Ramelli, "Sex Offenders Must Get Used to Public Scrutiny," *Honolulu Star-Bulletin*, May 31, 1997.

6. National Victim Center, "Community Notification of the Release of Sex Offenders," *Victims' Rights Sourcebook: A Compilation and Comparison of Victims' Rights Laws*. Arlington, VA: National Victim Center, 1996.

"Community notification laws give parents a false sense of security and often result in vigilantism and violence."

Community Notification Laws Do Not Prevent Child Abuse

Community notification laws were established as a response to the number of child sexual abuse cases involving repeat offenders. Community notification laws require sex offenders to register personal information with their local law enforcement and allow state officials and local citizens to notify their community that a sex offender resides in their neighborhood. Although the motivation for these laws is understandable, unfortunately they are not very effective in preventing child abuse.

Instead of actively preventing child abuse, community notification laws give parents a false sense of security and often result in vigilantism and violence when parents are notified that a convicted sexual offender has been released. Another problem with community notification laws is that sexual offenders are never given a chance to change their ways. Isolated and rejected by unforgiving neighbors, they are vulnerable to falling back into deviant behavior. Obviously this effect does little to prevent child abuse.

One of the most prominent community notification laws, Megan's Law, was named for seven-year-old Megan Kanka, who was molested and strangled by a repeat sex offender. Megan's Law is facing legal difficulties, according to *Newsweek* reporter Matt Bai: "Legal challenges persist, and an early study found that while chronic child molesters are less likely to get away with their crimes under the law, they're no less liable to commit them."[1]

No Solutions Are Offered

Megan's Law renders anyone who has ever made a mistake involving a child an instant monster. There appears to be no possibility of making up for their wrongdoing or even being given a modicum of dignity as a human being. Even after an offender has served his sentence for the crime, he continues to be punished if he attempts to rejoin society. This may satisfy the anger of those who have been personally affected by child abuse, but it hardly does any good toward preventing further incidents.

If anything, community notification laws can eventually lead to more incidents of child abuse. A former sex offender trying to lead a reformed and productive life may be barred from doing this by unsympathetic neighbors. If he's ostracized from society and forced to live underground, there's a good chance that the sex offender will commit his crime again because he feels so alienated from his community. "Making life-time lepers out of most all sex offenders could cripple the recovery of many and irrevocably some. Such tramplings that make sport out of destroying people will most certainly not reduce reoffense rates, it only sets a stage for further irre-sponsibility,"[2] argues the National Center on Institutions and Alternatives (NCIA).

An intolerant community prevents a person from ever becoming a responsible member of society and also promotes vigilantism. For example, when residents in one California town were notified of the release of a convicted sex offender, they responded by firebombing his car. In the state of Washington, an angry mob burned down the house of a known sex offender. This kind of behavior hardly seems appropriate, let alone lawful; it is exactly the behavior community notification laws are supposed to foil. Says NCIA, "Widespread Community Notification that makes dartboards out of sex offenders is risky business. We shouldn't be damning people and we shouldn't be making an outcast or pariah of anyone. Setting any group up to be hassled, hunted, or taunted is not the way to have less crime."[3]

Mistakes Can Happen

In addition to misguided harm to convicted sex offenders, community notification laws present dangers to completely innocent adults. There can be glitches in the laws: In one incident in Kansas, a family unknowingly moved into the previous home of a sex offender whose address was posted on the Internet through the Kansas Bureau of Investigation's sex offender registry. Because the addresses were not kept current, this innocent family was unfairly targeted as sex offenders, their home pelted with rocks and the children taunted.

Mistakes like the Kansas incident indicate that instead of preventing child abuse, innocent adults and children may become new victims of inaccurate information. "A 1994 federal law requiring states to establish registries of convicted sexual predators and child molesters apparently doesn't require those states to verify the offenders' addresses. This has had repercussions for innocent victims,"[4] says Henry Risley, deputy secretary of the Kansas Department of Corrections.

Politics Plays a Part

If community notification laws are not preventing child abuse and are not conducive to convicted offender rehabilitation, who is benefiting from the laws? The Libertarian Party alleges that politicians have the most to gain and that Megan's Law protects politicians' jobs rather than protecting children's lives. "When politicians talk about community notification, what they really mean is: 'We've just set more child rapists free in your neighborhood,'"[5] says party chairman Steve Dasbach.

Dasbach believes that the ineffective but highly publicized community notification laws help politicians create the false image that they are effecting positive changes toward increased child safety. For political rhetoric to be especially forceful, politicians also tend to perpetuate the notion that child abuse is everywhere, including decent neighborhoods. Community notification often contributes to this scare, terrorizing parents and provoking vigilantism.

Finally, wealthier neighborhoods are more vigilant about applying community notification laws. Richer communities also have better and better-funded resources to keep track of sex offenders. Thus richer communities tend to drive out offenders from their neighborhoods, leaving the poorer neighborhoods open to the offender. Since poor neighborhoods can sometimes have trouble providing school textbooks let alone updated information on local sex offenders, the result is that richer children receive more protection than those struggling in poverty. Clearly this is a flawed approach to reducing child sexual abuse.

Facing Change

The public is rightly afraid for their children, but confronting offenders with violence and acting on pure passion will not prevent the abuse of children. "Public notification is a quick fix to a highly emotional issue," according to Robert E. Freeman-Longo of the Safer Society Foundation. "Public notification may soothe local fears but it will not stop the known offender who wants to reoffend from going to an unsuspecting, neighboring community and selecting a victim."[6] New measures must be established to tackle the problem of child abuse head-on.

The laws do not offer long-term changes, which does not

go far in preventing child abuse on a permanent basis. Additionally, the laws do not address the majority of child abuse cases, which are perpetrated by family members, not strangers. How can community notification laws help the many victims of child abuse whose abuser lives right in the home? Since families hide their secrets well, chances are that children abused by parents will often be overlooked by adults in the community who are interested primarily in targeting obvious abusers. Being able to point out repeat offenders brings a sense of self-satisfaction to those who want to appear to be participating in the building of a strong community. The reality is that these highly visible actions do not get to the cause of the problem.

It is difficult to arrive at the root of the problem of child abuse, but it is clear that community notification laws are not the answer to protecting innocent children. If a community is to take genuine interest in its children and honestly wants to exert the effort it takes to combat such a complex problem, the quick-fix of community notification laws needs to be left behind for less simple, more individualized methods.

1. Matt Bai, "A Report from the Front in the War on Predators," *Newsweek*, May 19, 1997, p. 20.

2. National Center on Institutions and Alternatives, "Community Notification and Setting the Record Straight on Recidivism," November 8, 1996, www.igc.org/ncia/comnot.html.

3. National Center on Institutions and Alternatives, "Community Notification and Setting the Record Straight on Recidivism."

4. Henry Risley, "Is Your Neighbor a Sex Offender?" *Corrections Today*, August 1997, p. 86.

5. Libertarian Party, "Libertarians Ask: Will Megan's Law Protect Politicians—or Our Children?" *News from the Libertarian Party*, August 29, 1997, www.lp.org/rel/970829-Megan.html.

6. Robert E. Freeman-Longo, "Feel Good Legislation: Prevention or Calamity," *Child Abuse & Neglect*, February 1996, p. 98.

"Those who argue for giving sex offenders a second chance or the opportunity to redeem themselves in society probably do not have children of their own."

Punishing Child Molesters Will Reduce Child Abuse

People like Larry Don McQuay prove that child molesters are a different breed from the average human being. McQuay, who is in a Texas prison for molesting a six-year-old boy, claims to have molested more than two hundred children. He readily admits that he is not curable as a sexual offender and would undoubtedly repeat his offense if freed from prison. "I am doomed to eventually rape, then murder, my poor little victims to keep them from telling on me,"[1] he says. As horrifying as McQuay's words are, they provide society with a valuable warning to confront the problem of child sexual abuse in aggressive ways. Ultimately, the best way to deal with child molesters—with the purpose of reducing child abuse—is to punish them for their heinous behavior.

Child Molesters Are Usually Incurable

Child sexual abuse is spreading like a disease across the country, and there appears to be no cure. The Federal Bureau of Investigation estimates that one in four girls and one in six boys will be a victim of sexual abuse. However, fewer than one in twenty arrested sex offenders serve serious prison time. Ross Cheit, a professor of public policy, reports that 70 percent of convicted child molesters never actually serve time in jail. Cheit reveals, "Most people think that if found guilty of a felony sex offense against a child you'll serve serious time, but that is rarely the case."[2] Seventy-five percent of those who do spend time in prison go on to molest another child after being released. In other words, incorrigible sex offenders like McQuay are the norm but many of them are still free to commit heinous crimes.

The U.S. Department of Justice reports that offenders who served time for sexual assault were 7.5 times as likely as those convicted of other crimes to be rearrested for a new sexual assault. In a study carried out by the Bureau of Justice Statistics, of 109,000 prisoners released from prisons in 1983, at least 4,000 were rearrested for rape or sexual assault by 1986. This means that among the already high number of reported sexual abuse victims in those three years, at least 4,000 innocent people—mostly children—were victimized by criminals who had abused others before.

Studies repeatedly show that child sexual abusers cannot change. As former California governor Pete Wilson remarks, "Child molesters can't stop, because they have a compulsion to do what they do."[3] The National Institute of Justice concluded in a 1997 report that this sexual deviation is simply incurable, much like epilepsy or diabetes. This illness seems immune to the supposedly therapeutic effects of psychological treatment and rehabilitation programs.

Rehabilitation Does Not Work

When attempting to deal with child molesters, people are willing to consider rehabilitation. However, the sad truth is that rehabilitation does not work. Attorney and activist Andrew Vachss cites studies that indicate how useless rehabilitation is in changing sex offender behavior. For example, of the 767 rapists and child molesters included in a 1992

Minnesota study, "those who completed psychiatric treatment were arrested more often for new sex crimes than those who had not been treated at all."[4] Additionally, Vachss cites a Canadian study that tracked released child molesters for twenty years and showed that 43 percent abused again, regardless of the form or duration of rehabilitation. Says Vachss, "The difference between those simply incarcerated and those subjected to a full range of treatments appears to be statistically negligible. And the more violent and sadistic the offense, the more likely it is to be repeated."[5]

Rehabilitation simply fails to adequately confront the terrible problem of child sexual abuse. In an exhaustive study, researcher Robert Martinson examined every rehabilitation technique available in publication and found that "with few and isolated exceptions, the rehabilitative efforts that have been reported so far have had no appreciable effect on recidivism [the tendency of criminals to repeat their crime]."[6] In addition, rehabilitation drains taxpayer money, wastes people's time, and endangers innocent young lives. Instead of providing ineffective rehabilitation programs for these criminals, who have better provisions than the many neglected children who suffer in poverty, punitive measures are called for.

A Generous Punishment

There are effective forms of punishment that penalize sex offenders with permanent monitoring but still allow a generous degree of freedom. For example, the system of close monitoring of released inmates from Maricopa County, Arizona, has been effective in reducing the number of child sexual abuse incidents. A three-year study of nearly 1,100 Maricopa County sex offenders on lifetime probation found that only 1.5 percent repeated the offense. One forty-four-year-old man who had molested his stepdaughter from ages nine to twelve has been released into lifetime probation after serving a year in jail. For his degree of freedom, the sexual felon must undergo court-ordered individual and group therapy, and be available to surveillance officers checking in on his home without advance notice.

The convicted child molester must also "pass periodic tests that use a plethysmograph, which is attached to his penis, to measure the appropriateness of his physical responses to three-minute audiotapes describing, among other things, scenes with prepubescent girls,"[7] according to journalist Mike Tharp in *U.S. News & World Report.* These restrictions on child molesters are actually modest compared with measures many parents of sexually abused children would like to take.

Liberals argue that child molesters need to be treated "decently," which usually amounts to setting them free to attack again. That careless attitude is partially to blame for the spread of child sexual abuse in today's morally undisciplined society. The truth is, punishing child molesters for their terrible crimes does not mean indecent treatment. In fact, society has an obligation to punish offenders and teach them how decent people behave. Additionally, society should feel responsible for the children whose decency has been violated. The only way to get back to a decent society, which entails reducing child abuse effectively, is to punish child molesters. Often that punishment needs to be severe.

What About Chemical Castration?

Because child molesters do not respond well to rehabilitation, drastic measures must be considered. In 1996 Pete Wilson signed legislation that made California the first state in the nation to require chemical castration of repeat child molesters. This is a sensible move toward preventing uncontrollable criminals from acting on their sick impulses. It should be made clear that the law mandates chemical castration as a condition of parole. Essentially, it is allowing freedom to people who have violated innocent children and providing them with a tool to make sure they don't repeat their heinous crimes. This can hardly be considered harsh punishment.

The term *castration* has frightening connotations to many people. In actuality, chemical castration does not involve cutting off any body parts. Chemical castration is a drug treatment that is regularly administered to inhibit the production of the hormone testosterone. When testosterone levels drop, so too does the sex drive. Just as people go to the doctor for medication for medical conditions, child molesters can quite easily endure this relatively simple treatment for the sake of the innocent. Studies in Europe have shown that chemical castration decreased the rate of relapse of sex offenders. In Denmark, where twenty-six prisoners were given injections since 1989, only one of sixteen released went on to commit another offense. "My sex fantasies, which once made me a criminal, are gone,"[8] said Arne Kjeldson, a Danish inmate undergoing chemical castration.

Punishment Makes a Statement

Swift and definite punishment makes the most sense in a society plagued by unstoppable child molesters. Those who argue for giving sex offenders a second chance or the opportunity to redeem themselves in society probably do not have children of their own. If they did, they would not be so willing to use vulnerable children as part of a futile social experiment. As editor Chandra Hayslett says, "Why give these criminals a second chance to prove they can live in a society and not sexually abuse little, innocent children? Whose children will be the ones to make the first-time offenders into repeat offenders?"[9] Empathy, so freely doled out to these monsters, should be reserved for children and their parents. The most important issue is not how punishment affects child molesters but how certain punishments will keep children safe.

Failing to punish child molesters sends negative messages on varying levels. It tells children that their lives are in constant jeopardy and that no one really cares about their safety. It suggests to parents that their very real concerns for their children are secondary. Finally, it shows society that people can get away with child molestation, making the heinous act seem unimportant. If, as some so loudly claim, society wants to do the right thing to reduce child abuse, the first definite move must be to punish child molesters for their sick behavior.

1. "Child Molester Could Be Released," *Collegian*, April 3, 1996, www.spub.ksu.edu/issues/v100/sp/n123/ap-molesterrelease-17.html.

2. Quoted in Richard P. Morin, "Ross Cheit Seeks More Accurate Analysis of Child Molestation Data," *George Street Journal*, March 7, 1997, www.brown.edu/Administration/George_Street_Journal/cheit.html.

3. Quoted in Donna Alvarado, "Close-up: California Mandates Chemical Castration," *Seattle Times*, September 18, 1996, www.seattletimes.com/extra/browse/html/altcast_091896.html.

4. Andrew Vachss, "Sex Predators Can't Be Saved," *New York Times*, January 5, 1993.

5. Vachss, "Sex Predators Can't Be Saved."

6. Quoted in National Center for Policy Analysis, "Does Punishment Deter?" *NCPA Policy Backgrounder*, August 17, 1998.

7. Mike Tharp, "Tracking Sexual Impulses," *U.S. News & World Report*, July 7, 1997, www.usnews.com/usnews/issue/970707/7sex.htm.

8. Quoted in Katherine Seligman, "Chemical Castration May Not Work, Cost a Bundle," *San Francisco Examiner*, September 18, 1996.

9. Chandra M. Hayslett, "Castration Remedies Problem of Sex Crimes," *Daily Beacon*, August 28, 1996.

"Society must come up with better ways of dealing with child molesters, not simply incarcerate offenders and forget they exist."

Rehabilitating Child Molesters Will Reduce Child Abuse

Child molestation is considered one of the most heinous crimes a member of society can commit. People express horror at the mention of such atrocities whenever another tragic case makes its way onto the pages of the newspapers. Author Philip Jenkins reveals that in the eyes of today's general public, child molesters are "virtually unstoppable, either by repeated incarcerations or by prolonged programs of treatment or therapy, because their acts arose not from any temporary or reversible weakness of character but from a deep-rooted sickness or moral taint."[1] Such a horrible view of the perpetrator is not surprising considering the permanent trauma suffered by the victims. But as justified as the portrayal may seem, it is not entirely accurate.

They're Still Human Beings

Most child molesters are not "virtually unstoppable," as fear-ridden communities often think. In fact, "With or without treatment, the vast majority of once-caught sex offenders don't go on to be rearrested for a subsequent new sex offense,"[2] according to the National Center on Institutions and Alternatives. What many people do not know is that sex offenders have a lower recidivism rate than most other criminals, with approximately 13 percent committing another sex offense. Although this percentage still warrants concern, the point is that the terrible behavior is not uncontrollable.

Rather than suffering from a "deep-rooted sickness or moral taint," child molesters often abuse because they themselves were victims of sexual abuse. While this does not excuse the offender's act, it does help explain how it is possible for a human being to violate another human being. According to Gail Ryan, director of the Perpetration Prevention Project, "For those perpetrators who were sexually abused, early offenses sometimes appear to be reenactments of their own victimization."[3] The child molester is frequently a sad casualty in the cycle of violence that harms innocent children and

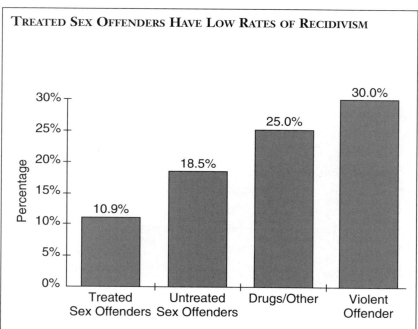

TREATED SEX OFFENDERS HAVE LOW RATES OF RECIDIVISM

Source: Margaret Alexander, "Sex OffendersTreatment: A Response to Furby et al.," *Meta-Analysis*, 1994.

sometimes turns them into someone else's tormentor. With that understanding, it seems clear that rehabilitation, not punishment, is the best mode of dealing with child molesters, people who are not so far from the norm as most people would prefer to think.

Rehabilitation Does Not Mean Forgetting

People appear to think that rehabilitation of child molesters means forgiving the terrible harm they've done and then letting them go free. In fact, rehabilitation rarely means freedom for the offender. Instead, it involves making sure the offenders understand the full extent of their harmful behavior and pay their debt to society. Child molesters are committed to facilities where their rehabilitation is enforced. In the long run, this deters deviant behavior and is conducive to positive social change.

One good example of uniquely effective rehabilitation programs is the Snake River Correctional Institution in Oregon. The program operates under the philosophy that "sex offenders are completely responsible for their behaviors and that treatment must continue to focus on the offender taking responsibility for his/her behavior."[4] The facility is officially a prison, but it is distinguished from other prisons in its emphasis on treatment to effect long-term changes in the inmates. For example, one facet of the program requires the completion of a two-week sex offender orientation class, addressing issues such as criminal thinking and sex offender treatment methods and models. This allows offenders the chance to feel responsible for changing their own thoughts and behavior.

Preventing a Future of Child Abuse

Says Gail Ryan, "Treatment of abusers is not an act of compassion in and of itself, and yet its goal must be to model compassionate behavior. . . . Effective interventions must be both therapeutic and correctional, the therapist and the court exercising both empathy and accountability."[5] The immediate disgust most people feel at the mention of child molestation often overrides a social obligation to be fair about the treatment of offenders. The common reaction is to apply forceful punishment, which may satisfy those who are outraged by the offender's behavior but does very little toward changing destructive behavior.

Punishing is a reaction, an admission that society merely reacts to bad things instead of preventing them in the first place. Rehabilitation is proactive as well as reactive, a positive way for society to take charge of negative situations and transform them for the benefit of the community. Rehabilitation also can contribute to the goal of reducing child abuse by utilizing the offender's experience to educate children and parents. Thus, cycles of violence can sometimes be broken. "Addressing the psychological harm done to offenders in the past may help to reduce the harm they inflict on others in the future, thus preempting intergenerational cycles of abuse,"[6] says Eric Lotke of the National Center on Institutions and Alternatives.

Complex Relationships

Rehabilitation is preferable to punishment in light of the fact that child sexual abuse is usually not a random act of violence. "Despite the onslaught of publicity surrounding crimes committed by sexually violent strangers, the devastating truth is that most child sexual abuse is committed by a relative or friend of the victim,"[7] says legal expert Cynthia King. Punishment cannot begin to repair the damage the child experiences personally and in his or her relationship with family members, including the perpetrator. Punishing a father or grandfather will not take away the pain that the victim continues to feel after the sexual abuse is stopped. If the perpetrator does not acknowledge his own responsibility, the victim continues to suffer emotional abuse throughout childhood and into adulthood.

Rehabilitation provides a complex answer to complex problems. For example, Sharon Simone, who won a civil suit against her father some thirty years after he had abused her as a child, says that after a time of family divisions, denials, and anger, her father finally admitted his wrongs and entered treatment. The rehabilitating treatment, not drastic punishment like chemical castration, helped heal the father as well as Simone. Her own son witnessed the honesty and acceptance of responsibility between his mother and grandfather, and "was an intimate part of it," says Simone. "He's the next generation. He said he is not going to hold a grudge. He's not ashamed to talk about his family history and its legacy. He said that legacy would end with him."[8] Hence, rehabilitation has long-term beneficial effects.

Child sexual abuse is a tragedy that must be confronted until there are no more incidents to address. But society must come up with better ways of dealing with child molesters, not simply incarcerate offenders and forget they exist. It hardly does children good to know that child molesters are simply locked away, ready to pounce on innocent kids if they escape their prison cells. This teaches children that long-term solutions for creating a safer environment can be avoided by locking up the problem. Rehabilitation is the best way to provide children and the rest of society with a sense of security and to prevent further abuse.

1. Philip Jenkins, *Moral Panic: Changing Concepts of the Child Molester in Modern America.* New Haven, CT: Yale University Press, 1998, p. 189.

2. National Center on Institutions and Alternatives, "Community Notification and Setting the Record Straight on Recidivism," November 8, 1996, www.igc.org/ncia/comnot.html.

3. Gail Ryan, "The Sexual Abuser," in Mary Edna Helfer, Ruth S. Kempe, and Richard D. Krugman, eds., *The Battered Child.* Chicago: University of Chicago Press, 1997, p. 330.

4. Quoted in Thomas L. Lester, "Sex Offender Facility Committed to Change and Rehabilitation," *Corrections Today,* April 1995, p. 168.

5. Ryan, "The Sexual Abuser," p. 343.

6. Eric Lotke, "Sex Offenders: Does Treatment Work?" *Issues and Answers*, 1996, www.igc.org/ncia/sexo.html.

7. Cynthia A. King, "Fighting the Devil We Don't Know: *Kansas v. Hendricks:* A Case Study Exploring the Civilization of Criminal Punishment and Its Effectiveness in Preventing Child Sexual Abuse," *William and Mary Law Review*, April 1999, p. 1,429.

8. Sharon Simone, "Salem, Massachusetts 'Day of Contrition,'" *Facing the Issues: Grief and Mourning*, January 14, 1997, www.yesican.org/articles/salem.html.

APPENDIX A

FACTS ABOUT CHILD ABUSE

- In 1997, over 3 million reports of child abuse and neglect were received by child protective service agencies in the United States.
- In 1997, the incidence of reports of child abuse was 47 per 1,000 children in the U.S. population.
- Child abuse reporting levels increased 41 percent between 1988 and 1997.
- Child protective service agencies investigate more than 2 million reports alleging maltreatment of children each year. In 1997, 1 million children were identified as victims of substantiated abuse or neglect, an 18 percent increase from 1990.
- Confirmed cases of child maltreatment in 1997 included 22 percent physical abuse, 8 percent sexual abuse, 54 percent neglect, 4 percent emotional abuse, and 12 percent other forms of maltreatment.
- Every day in the United States, 3 or more children die as a result of child abuse or neglect.
- Approximately 1,195 children die from maltreatment each year.
- The rate of child abuse fatalities increased by 34 percent between 1985 and 1997.
- Between 1995 and 1997, 78 percent of child fatalities were children age five or younger and 38 percent were under one year of age.
- Of child fatalities in 1997, 44 percent resulted from neglect, 51 percent from physical abuse, and 5 percent from a combination of neglectful and physically abusive parenting.
- Approximately 41 percent of child fatalities in 1997 involved children who were known to child protective services as current or prior clients.
- In 1997, approximately 84,320 new cases of child sexual abuse were opened, accounting for 8 percent of all confirmed victims.
- Every hour 17 children are sexually abused in the United States.
- An estimated 1 in 4 girls and 1 in 6 boys will be sexually abused by age 18.

- Girls are sexually abused three times more often than boys, and boys have a greater risk of emotional neglect and of serious injury than girls.
- Of confirmed child abuse victims in 1996, 53 percent were white, 27 percent African American, 11 percent Hispanic, 2 percent American Indian/Alaska Native, and 1 percent Asian American/Pacific Islander.
- Based on information from 18 states, reports of abuse in daycare, foster care, or other institutional care settings represent about 3 percent of all confirmed cases. This percentage has remained consistent over the past eleven years.
- Approximately 77 percent of child abusers are parents and 11 percent are other relatives of the victim.
- 70 percent to 85 percent of sexual abuse offenders are known by the child.
- 80 percent of all child abuse perpetrators are under age 40.
- Almost two-thirds of perpetrators are female.
- An estimated three-fourths of neglect and medical neglect cases are associated with female perpetrators, while almost three-fourths of sexual abuse cases are associated with male perpetrators.
- Children in single-parent households have a 77 percent greater risk of being physically abused, an 87 percent greater risk of being neglected, and an 80 percent greater risk of suffering serious injury from maltreatment than children living with both parents.
- Children from the lowest income families are 18 times more likely to be sexually abused and 22 times more likely to be seriously injured from maltreatment.

APPENDIX B

Excerpts from Related Documents

Document 1: Prevalence of Different Types of Maltreatment
The National Committee to Prevent Child Abuse performed a fifty-state survey of the number and characteristics of child abuse reports. This selection describes the different types of child maltreatment found most commonly in the United States.

To provide appropriate prevention and treatment services, it is necessary to determine the prevalence of different types of maltreatment as well as other characteristics of the CPS caseload. Each state liaison was asked to provide a breakdown of all reported and substantiated cases by type of maltreatment for 1996 and 1997. Five categories were provided: physical abuse, sexual abuse, neglect, emotional maltreatment and other. Twenty-one states provided reporting data for both years while 30 states gave a breakdown for substantiated cases for both years. Although most of the states were able to provide data using the above-mentioned categories, a few states did not distinguish emotional maltreatment from neglect while three states included sexual abuse in the category of physical abuse.

Neglect represents the most common type of reported and substantiated form of maltreatment. In 1997, 22 states provided the following breakdown for reported cases: 52% involved neglect, 26% physical abuse, 7% sexual abuse, 4% emotional maltreatment and 11% other. For substantiated cases, 31 states gave the following breakdowns: 54% neglect, 22% physical abuse, 8% sexual abuse, 4% emotional maltreatment and 12% other. Compared to the reported cases, the substantiated cases contain a slightly higher percentage of neglect and a slightly lower percentage of physical abuse cases. Similar to the pattern observed between 1994 and 1996, these two distributions are almost identical. However, it is noted that "other" has become a bigger category in 1997 for both reported and substantiated cases than in previous years. This reflects that states are using more detailed systems in classifying types of child maltreatment. For example, behaviors included under the "other" category are abandonment, multiple types of maltreatment, imminent risk, medical and educational neglect, substance and alcohol abuse, dependency, threat of harm, and lack of supervision or bizarre discipline.

In the 1980's and early 1990's, the greatest difference between the reported and substantiated distributions involved sexual abuse and neglect cases. Overall, substantiated cases tended to include a larger percentage of sexual abuse and a lower percentage of child neglect than was observed in the larger pool of all reports. The similarity in the distribution of reported and substantiated cases in terms of primary type of abuse suggest that type of abuse, alone, may not be as critical a factor as in the past in determining whether a case will be substantiated. Neglect cases are now as likely to be substantiated as cases involving other forms of maltreatment.

The types of cases most frequently reported to child protective services have undergone some shift between 1985 and 1996, potentially reflecting a change in the type of cases professionals and the public are willing to report to CPS and the classification systems used by child welfare systems in describing the reports they do receive. One of the most interesting shifts suggested by these patterns is the decline in the proportion of reported cases involving child sexual abuse. While such cases represented 16% of all reports in 1986, this percentage has gradually declined over the years. In the most recent survey, sexual abuse cases were only 7% of all reports. To a certain extent, the rapid increase in the number of reported cases of child sexual abuse observed in the mid to late 1980's reflected the increased awareness and attention to a form of maltreatment which had been virtually ignored prior to this time. Child welfare agencies across the country were inundated with cases, many of which had involved several years of ongoing abuse. After over ten years of attention to this problem, it is possible that the reservoir of cases involving years of abuse have been so reduced such that child welfare is less burdened with such cases. Further, improvements in professional practice and the rapid expansion of child assault prevention services have produced an environment in which cases are identified closer to the onset of the abuse.

Whatever the reason, the decline in the percentage of reported cases involving child sexual abuse coupled with the changes in the pattern of substantiated cases noted above has resulted in a continued downward trend in the number of sexual abuse cases currently on CPS caseloads. Looking at the absolute number of child sexual abuse cases substantiated by the 30 states which are able to provide us this information for both reporting periods, the number of such cases dropped 3% between 1996 and 1997. Nationwide, we estimate that approximately 84,320 new cases of child sexual abuse were accepted for service last year. While significantly lower than the absolute number of cases accepted in the first part of this decade, this number is far higher than the 10,000 to 20,000 cases of child sexual abuse cases served in the 1970's and early 1980's. It underscores the substantial threat to child well being represented by this form of maltreatment.

National Committee to Prevent Child Abuse, *Current Trends in Child Abuse Reporting and Fatalities: The Results of the 1997 Annual Fifty State Survey.* Chicago: Prevent Child Abuse America, 1998.

Document 2: Characteristics of Perpetrators of Child Abuse and Neglect

In this excerpt from its comprehensive study of the incidence of child abuse and neglect, the National Center on Child Abuse and Neglect quantifies and qualifies some of the major characteristics of child abusers.

Children who had been maltreated as defined by the Harm Standard were categorized according to their relationship to the most closely related perpetrator and according to this perpetrator's sex, age, and employment status; these categorizations were examined in relation to the type of maltreatment and the severity of the child's injury or harm. Perpetrators' relationships to the children also were examined in relation to the children's race. The findings represent only a preliminary exploration of perpetrator characteristics in the NIS-3 data, since they lack significance tests concerning potential relationships and substantial percentages of the children were missing information concerning certain of the perpetrator characteristics.

Perpetrator's Relationship to the Child. The majority of all children countable under the Harm Standard (78%) were maltreated by their birth parents, and this held true both for children who were abused (62% were maltreated by birth parents) and for those who were neglected (91% experienced neglect by birth parents).

Birth parents were the most closely related perpetrators for 72 percent of the physically abused children and for 81 percent of the emotionally abused children. The pattern was distinctly different for sexual abuse. Nearly one-half of the sexually abused children were sexually abused by someone other than a parent or parent-substitute, while just over one-fourth were sexually abused by a birth parent, and one-fourth were sexually abused by other than a birth parent or parent-substitute. In addition, a sexually abused child was most likely to sustain a serious injury or impairment when a birth parent was the perpetrator.

Perpetrator's Sex. Children were somewhat more likely to be maltreated by female perpetrators than by males: 65 percent of the maltreated children had been maltreated by a female, whereas 54 percent had been maltreated by a male. Of children who were maltreated by their birth parents, the majority (75%) were maltreated by their mothers and a sizable minority (46%) were maltreated by their fathers (some children were maltreated by both parents). In contrast, children who were maltreated by other parents or parent-substitutes, or by other persons, were more likely to have been maltreated by a male than by a female (80 to 85% were maltreated by males; 14 to 41% by females).

Abused children presented a different pattern in connection with the sex of their perpetrators than did the neglected children. Children were more often neglected by female perpetrators (87% by females versus 43% by males). This finding is congruent with the fact that mothers and mother-substitutes tend to be the primary caretakers and are the primary persons held accountable for any omissions and/or failings in caretaking. In contrast, children were more often abused by males (67% were abused by males versus 40% by females). The prevalence of male perpetrators was strongest in the category of sexual abuse, where 89 percent of the children were abused by a male compared to only 12 percent by a female.

Among all abused children, those abused by their birth parents were about equally likely to have been abused by mothers as by fathers (50% and 58%, respectively), but those abused by other parents, parent-substitutes, or other, nonparental perpetrators were much more likely to be abused by males (80 to 90% by males versus 14 to 15% by females). This general pattern held for emotional abuse, but was slightly different in the area of physical abuse. Children who had been physically abused by their birth parents were more likely to have suffered at the hands of their mothers than their fathers (60% versus 48%), while those who had been physically abused by other parents or parent-substitutes were much more likely to have been abused by their fathers or father-substitutes (90% by their fathers versus 19% by their mothers). For sexual abuse, the child's relationship to the perpetrator made very little difference, since males clearly predominated as perpetrators, whatever their relationship to the child. Moreover, the severity of the injury or impairment that the child experienced as a result of maltreatment did not appear to bear any relationship to the sex of the perpetrator.

Perpetrator's Age. The perpetrator's age was entirely unknown for one-third of the children who were countable under the Harm Standard. Given the prevalence of children maltreated by perpetrators of unknown age, the findings here are tentative, since they could easily be eradicated if all perpetrators' ages were known.

Among all maltreated children, only a small percentage (13%) had been maltreated by a perpetrator in the youngest age bracket (under 26 years of age). However, younger perpetrators were slightly more predominant among children who had been sexually abused (where 22% had been sexually abused by a perpetrator under 26 years of age) and among children who had been maltreated in any way by someone who was not their parent or parent-substitute (among whom 40% had been maltreated by a perpetrator in the youngest age bracket).

A child's severity of injury or harm from maltreatment appeared not to be associated with the age of the perpetrator.

Perpetrator's Employment Status. Perpetrator's employment status was unknown for more than one-third of the maltreated children, limiting the value of the findings on this issue. Nearly one-half of all maltreated children were abused by a perpetrator who was employed, and this held true for both abuse and neglect. Of the children who sustained serious injury, the majority were maltreated by an employed perpetrator. In no category were the majority of children maltreated by a perpetrator who was unemployed.

Child's Race and Relationship to the Perpetrator. Because the perpetrator's race was not known for children submitted to the study solely through non-CPS sources, the child's race was examined in connection with the relationship to the perpetrator and with the nature and severity of the maltreatment.

For overall abuse, child's race reflected no notable connection to the relationship with the perpetrator. However, among sexually abused children, white children constituted a greater proportion of children who were sexually abused by their birth parents than of those sexually abused by other parents and parent-substitutes, and by others. Among physically abused children, white children were more prevalent among those who were physically abused by other parents and parent-substitutes than among those who were physically abused by their birth parents or among those physically abused by other types of perpetrators. Although non-white children were the minority of victims in all categories, they were more prevalent among children who were physically or sexually abused by perpetrators other than parents or parent-substitutes.

White children are a larger majority of those who suffered serious injury, whereas non-white children's representation was strongest among those who experienced moderate injury and among those for whom injury could be inferred based on the severity of their maltreatment.

National Center on Child Abuse and Neglect, *Executive Summary of the Third National Incidence Study of Child Abuse and Neglect.* Washington, DC: U.S. Department of Health and Human Services, 1996.

Document 3: Munchausen Syndrome by Proxy

In this excerpt from a guide for investigators of child abuse, the Office of Juvenile Justice and Delinquency Prevention describes a peculiar form of child abuse, Munchausen syndrome by proxy, in which an abusive parent brings a child into the hospital for frequent and unaccountable illnesses.

Munchausen syndrome by proxy (MSBP) is a form of child abuse wherein a parent (usually the mother) intentionally fabricates illness in her child and repeatedly presents the child for medical care, disclaiming knowledge as to the cause of the problem. Child victims of MSBP are at risk for serious injury or death.

Diagnostic Criteria

MSBP occurs when there is:

• Illness in a child that is simulated (faked) or produced by a parent or other caretaker, or both.

• Presentation of the child for medical assessment and care, usually persistently, often resulting in multiple medical procedures.

• Denial of knowledge by the parent as to the cause of the child's illness.

• Subsiding of acute symptoms and signs when the child is separated from the parent.

Typically, but not always, the mother spends a good deal of time on the hospital ward with the child and exhibits a remarkable familiarity with medical terminology. She may be "confidentially friendly" with the hospital staff, although she may show frustration with her child's chronic illness and anger at the medical staff's inadequate vigor in pursuing her child's problems. She may insist that she is the "only one" for whom the child will eat, drink, or swallow medicines.

If more than one child in a family dies of sudden infant death syndrome (SIDS) or of any other ill-defined disease, MSBP—that is, homicide—along with some genetic, metabolic, environmental, and toxicological causes of death, must be considered as more likely explanations. . . .

Investigation

A multidisciplinary child protection team should become involved early on. The team should include medical personnel, the primary care nurse, county social services, mental health professionals, and an epidemiologist (a person who, in part, specializes in figuring out the cause of disease). Together, they must determine if the child's medical condition can be attributed to MSBP, warranting civil proceedings to remove the child from the perpetrator's care and, possibly, criminal proceedings. Police and law enforcement personnel should become involved early in a case. Evidence collection, timely arrest, and development of a case for prosecution are some of their roles.

Records to Examine

• The hospital's medical records for the child. They may be so voluminous that a summary and analysis will have to be prepared for the use of the investigators. Medical records should always be reviewed by medical doctors, so that information is not misinterpreted.

• Medical records (preferably originals) from other institutions.

• All medical records of all siblings, including autopsy reports and death certificates.

• The parents' educational and work history.

Part of the investigation will include an interview with the primary care nurse in the hospital, for this person is often the one who has spent the most time with the child and the parent during multiple hospitalizations. This person, and others interviewed, may be nonpartisan about the possibility of MSBP or may deny it vehemently, insisting on the mother's good care of the child. Investigators should never divulge information to the person they are interviewing.

Either the pediatrician or the multidisciplinary team as a body will make the final diagnosis of MSBP, based on the facts, discrepancies between these and the mother's various accounts, and a determination of whether the discrepancies are the result of misunderstanding, incapacity, or fabrication.

Office of Juvenile Justice and Delinquency Prevention, *Child Neglect and Munchausen Syndrome by Proxy*.Washington, DC: Office of Juvenile Justice and Delinquency Prevention, 1996.

Document 4: Parental Child Abduction Is Child Abuse

Nancy Faulkner argues that parental kidnapping, on the increase in recent decades, should be considered child abuse because of the serious emotional and sometimes physical trauma sustained by abducted children.

Post-divorce parental child stealing has been on the increase since the mid-1970s, paralleling the rising divorce rate and the escalating litigation over child custody (Huntington, 1986). According to Hoff (1997), "The term 'parental kidnapping' encompasses the taking, retention or conceal-ment of a child by a parent, other family member, or their agent, in dero-gation of the custody rights, including visitation rights, of another parent or family member."

The abductor parent may move from one state to another, beginning a new round of investigation into the abuse with each move, impeding inter-vention by child protective services (Jones, Lund & Sullivan, 1996). Or, the abductor may flee to another country, completely shutting down any hopes of involvement by child protective services in the country of origin. The most pervasive scenario is that the abducting parent goes into hiding, or moves beyond the jurisdiction of governing law.

"These kidnappings are very cleverly plotted and planned and often involve the assistance of family members. The target parent has no for-warding address or telephone numbers." (Clawar & Rivlin, p. 115)

Huntington and others believe that inherent in the act of kidnapping and concealment are negative consequences for the child victims. It is Huntington's contention that one of the most concerning factors is that the parent has fled and "is out of reach of law and child protection agen-cies." To escape discovery the abductor parent is hiding out—"so who knows what is happening with [the] child!" (Huntington, 1982).

The abducted child is without the safeguards normally provided by child law. This leaves the child completely vulnerable to the dictates of the abductor parent, who, as evidenced in the following research by Johnson and Girdner, may not have the child's best interests in mind, or may be functioning with severe impediments. . . .

Children who have been psychologically violated and maltreated through the act of abduction are more likely to exhibit a variety of psy-chological and social handicaps. These handicaps make them vulnerable to detrimental outside influences (Rand, 1997). Huntington (1982) lists some of the deleterious effects of parental child abduction on the child victim:

1. Depression;
2. Loss of community;
3. Loss of stability, security, and trust;
4. Excessive fearfulness, even of ordinary occurrences;
5. Loneliness;
6. Anger;
7. Helplessness;
8. Disruption in identity formation; and
9. Fear of abandonment.

Nancy Faulkner, "Parental Child Abduction Is Child Abuse," presented to the United Nations Convention on Child Rights, June 9, 1999, www.prevent-abuse-now.com/unreport.htm.

Document 5: The History of Child Abuse

Lloyd deMause posits that child abuse has a long and universal history, dating back to antiquity and emerging in a variety of ways in modern times.

During the past three decades, I have spent much of my scholarly life examining primary historical sources such as diaries, autobiographies, doctor's reports and other documents that reveal what it must have felt like to have been a child—yesterday and today, in the East and the West, in literate and preliterate cultures.

In several hundred articles and books published by myself and my associates in *The Journal of Psychohistory* and elsewhere, we have documented extensive evidence that the history of childhood has been a nightmare from which we have only recently begun to awaken. The further back in history one goes—and the further away from the West one gets—the more massive the cruelty and neglect one finds and the more likely children are to have been killed, abandoned, beaten, terrorized and sexually abused by their caretakers.

Indeed, my conclusion from a lifetime of psychohistorical study of childhood and society is that the history of humanity is founded upon the abuse of children. Just as family therapists today find that child abuse often functions to hold families together as a way of solving their emotional problems, so, too, the routine assault of children has been society's most effective way of maintaining its collective emotional homeostasis. Most historical families once practiced infanticide, erotic beating and incest. Most states sacrificed and mutilated their children to relieve the guilt of adults. Even today, we continue to arrange the daily killing, maiming, molestation and starvation of children through our social, military and economic activities. . . .

The main psychological mechanism that operates in all child abuse involves using children as what I have termed *poison containers*—receptacles into which they project disowned parts of their psyches, so they can control these feelings in another body without danger to themselves. In *good* parenting, the child uses the *caretaker* as a poison container, much as it earlier used the mother's placenta as a poison container for cleansing its polluted blood. A good mother reacts with calming actions to the cries of a baby and helps it "detoxify" its dangerous emotions. But when an *immature* mother's baby cries, she cannot stand the screaming, and strikes out at the child. As one battering mother put it, "I have never felt loved all my life. When the baby was born, I thought he would love me. When he cried, it meant he didn't love me. So I hit him." Rather than the child being able to use the parent to detoxify its fears and anger, the parent instead injects his or her bad feelings into the child and uses it to cleanse him or herself of depression and anger.

Lloyd deMause, "The History of Child Abuse," speech, 1993, www.geocities.com/HotSprings/Spa/7173/ph-abuse.htm.

Document 6: A Child's Right to Live

This excerpt from Robert W. Ten Bensel, Marguerite M. Rheinberger, and Samuel X. Radbill's thorough illustration of violence against children throughout history shows how newborns' right to live has been in doubt.

In ancient times, when might was right, the infant had no rights until the right to live was ritually bestowed. Until then, the infant was a nonentity and could be disposed of with little compunction. The newborn had to be acknowledged by the father; what the father produced was his to do with as he wished. Proclaiming the child as his own not only assured life and welfare but also inheritance rights. Children's rights were also a prerogative of parenthood. As the head of the family, the father had the ultimate authority; even the mother was subordinate.

With some, the child was not really of this world until he or she had partaken of some earthly nourishment. A drop of milk or honey or even water could ensure life to the newborn. An eighth-century story tells of a grandmother who, outraged by her daughter-in-law's numerous brood of daughters, ordered the next-born daughter to be slain. Her servants kidnapped the baby—another girl—as soon as she was born, before she could be put to the mother's breast, and tried to drown her in a bucket of water. A merciful neighbor, however, rescued the infant and put a little honey in her mouth, which she promptly swallowed. The child was thus protected and her right to live assured. In British New Guinea, traditionally an infant was taken to the banks of a stream and the infant's lips moistened with water. The baby that did not accept the water was thrown away.

To determine fitness to live, the Germans would plunge the newborn into an icy river. This was done not only to toughen the child but to test its hardiness. Some North American Indians threw the newborn into a pool of water and saved it only if it rose to the surface and cried. Elsewhere there were other ordeals for survival.

In the Society Islands, a parent could not kill with impunity a child who had survived for a day; in some places, the child was safe even after a half-hour of survival.

The child was a nonperson in some societies until it received a name, which identified it as an individual. The Christian child was not granted full heavenly recognition until it was christened, at which time a "Christian" name was bestowed. The soul of a child that died before baptism was believed not to go to heaven but to be condemned to everlasting limbo. The body of such a child could not be buried in hallowed ground but instead was disposed of elsewhere.

Illegitimate children have long been outlawed and especially liable to abuse. "Born in sin," they were without benefit of clergy or inheritance. Illegitimate children were unwelcome, ostracized, and often abandoned or killed by their despondent mothers. If the babies survived, they were subject to degradation and maltreatment. The church offered protective institutions that hid the mothers' identity, hoping to encourage compromised mothers to spare their infants. A study in 1917 indicated that of the four to five thousand illegitimate children born in Chicago every year, one thousand disappeared completely. In 1915, Norway adopted a law that conferred rights upon such children—including the right to a father's name, to parental support, and to inheritance equal with that of siblings born in wedlock. Only within recent years has some alleviation from the stigma of illegitimacy been granted in the United States.

Robert W. Ten Bensel, Marguerite M. Rheinberger, and Samuel X. Radbill, "Children in a World of Violence: The Roots of Child Maltreatment," in Mary Edna Helfer, Ruth S. Kempe, and Richard D. Krugman, eds., *The Battered Child*. Chicago: University of Chicago Press, 1997.

Document 7: Spanking May Not Be So Bad After All

Lynn Rosellini declares that new studies have found that spanking does not carry the negative consequences that child-raising experts have claimed for years. Spanking is specified as a few swats, nothing harsher.

The notion advanced by a slew of American child-raising authorities that a couple of well-placed swats on the rear of your beloved preschooler irreparably harms him or her is essentially a myth. Antispanking crusaders relied on inconclusive studies to make sweeping overgeneralizations about spanking's dangers. Even the American Academy of Pediatrics is expected to tone down its blanket injunction against spanking, though it still takes a dim view of the practice and encourages parents to develop discipline alternatives. An AAP conference on corporal punishment in 1996 concluded that in certain circumstances, spanking may be an effective backup to other forms of discipline. "There's no evidence that a child who is spanked moderately is going to grow up to be a criminal or antisocial or violent," says S. Kenneth Schonberg, a pediatrics professor who co-chaired the conference. In fact, the reverse may be true: A few studies suggest that when used appropriately, spanking makes small children less likely to fight with others and more likely to obey their parents.

Some caveats are in order. By "spanking," the AAP and other authorities mean one or two flat-handed swats on a child's wrist or rear end, *not* a sustained whipping with Dad's belt. Neither the AAP nor any other child-development specialists believe that spanking should be the sole or preferred means of child discipline, or that it should be administered when a parent is very angry, or that it should be used with adolescents or children under 2 years old. Most experts who approve of spanking suggest it be used sparingly, as an adjunct to other discipline techniques.

Lynn Rosellini, "When to Spank," *U.S. News & World Report*, April 13, 1998.

Document 8: Cultural Tradition or Child Abuse?

African genital rites are considered child abuse in the United States, conflicting with the beliefs of many African immigrants. Some professional groups are attempting to address the issues from a culturally objective point of view, describes Celia W. Dugger.

Just six months after arriving in Houston from a Somalian refugee camp, Ahmed Guled's family has eased into the American mainstream. . . .

Guled himself holds dear the all-American dream that his children will go to college and prosper in the United States. But he also clings to an ancient tradition that is customary in parts of Africa—and that became a federal crime this year.

He believes his daughters must have their clitorises cut off and their genital lips stitched together to preserve their virginity and to follow what he believes his Muslim faith requires of him. . . .

Congress this year [1996] adopted a dual strategy to combat the practice in the United States. It directed federal health agencies to develop a plan to reach out to the immigrant communities and educate them about the harm of genital cutting. And it criminalized the practice, making it punishable by up to five years in prison. . . .

The law itself has been sharply debated among many Africans who have settled in the United States. Even some opposed to the practice say they are offended that Congress adopted a law that seems specifically directed at Africans, rather than relying on general statutes prohibiting violence against children, as France has done.

Others feel that Americans have unfairly stereotyped Africans as people who mutilate their children. . . .

Among Somali refugees resettled by the U.S. government in Houston, some say they will abandon the practice, while others say they must continue it.

Workers at the Refugee Services Alliance, an agency that helps settle refugees, say language barriers, cultural differences and poverty all conspire to isolate the refugees.

Celia W. Dugger, "Tug of Taboos: African Genital Rite vs. American Law," *New York Times*, December 28, 1996.

Document 9: Suffering Children and the Christian Science Church

Caroline Fraser, whose family adhered to Christian Science beliefs, explores the struggle between Christian Scientists' insistence on their right to refuse medical treatment for their children and the U.S. government's attempts to confront the number of child fatalities that have resulted directly from the church's practice.

In recent decades the Christian Science Church has succeeded in most states in establishing the right of Christian Scientists to deny their children medical treatment. Lobbyists have encouraged state legislatures to enact laws that protect Christian Scientists from prosecution for child abuse or neglect. These statutes provide a religious defense against such civil or criminal charges by stating that parents who rely solely on spiritual treatment in accordance with the beliefs of a recognized church are not considered to have failed to provide adequate care. Some stipulate that religious rights cannot limit a child's access to medical care in life-threatening situations; others do not. But none of them makes clear how parents who eschew medical care for their children can be trusted to distinguish illnesses that are life-threatening from those that are not.

The Church refuses to release any figures on its membership, but in 1989 a Church official told the *Los Angeles Times* that there were roughly 7,000 Christian Science children in this country. No national studies on the mortality of Christian Scientists have ever been done, but smaller studies have pointed to a high mortality rate among Christian Scientists—for example, among the graduates of Principia, the Christian Science college. The American Academy of Pediatrics and the American Medical Association have publicly declared their opposition to the laws that allow Christian Scientists and members of other religious groups to withhold medical care.

The Church rejects "faith healing" as a description of its proceedings, claiming that its "scientific" methods are not reliant on miracles and are nothing less than a rediscovery of the methods of Jesus Christ himself. Victor Westberg, the official spokesman of the Church, says, "We pray differently." But the dictionary definition of "faith healing" makes no such distinctions. Massage the rhetoric though they will, Christian Scientists practice faith healing as Webster's defines it: "a method or practice of treating diseases by prayer and exercise of faith in God." And the "verification" of these healings offered by the Church can be accepted only on faith. The Church's media guide claims that "Christian Science healing has been verified by medical diagnosis," and that of the more than 10,000 healings published from 1969 to 1988 in Church periodicals, 2,337 involved healings of conditions that had been medically diagnosed. Diagnosis, however, is not verification of healing, and the fact that a person recovers from an illness does not prove that Christian Science accomplished the recovery. The late Robert Peel, a Christian Science scholar, in his 1987 book *Spiritual Healing in a Scientific Age*, offered expanded anecdotal accounts of Christian Science healing. Some of these recoveries were verified, most of them indirectly and anecdotally, by physicians, but many of the physicians were not identified by name or institution, and only one physician (who withheld his name) expressed in writing his belief that Christian Science could heal. None of the participants were part of any kind of scientific study.

Caroline Fraser, "Suffering Children and the Christian Science Church," *Atlantic Monthly*, April 1995.

Document 10: The Suggestibility of Children

Old cases involving child abuse are being reconsidered in light of studies that indicate the high suggestibility of children when questioned by inconsistent therapists.

In the 1990s, researchers estimate, 500 studies have been conducted on children's "suggestibility"—the extent to which suggestions implanted by adult interviewers can influence children's recollections and accounts.

Though debate still burns high on some points—like the general level of children's accuracy and how resistant they are to disclosing that they have been abused—researchers describe an emerging consensus over how children should be interviewed to minimize false reports.

Warring camps of psychologists also appear to have reached broad agreement on this basic picture: The vast majority of the tens of thousands of child sexual abuse accusations each year are true, and most children display a tremendous capacity to be accurate; but under certain conditions, if they are pushed and prodded in the wrong ways, children may say false things. And preschoolers of 3 and 4 tend to be more suggestible than older children.

It was that body of research that underlay the Massachusetts Superior Court ruling by Judge Isaac Borenstein in June [1998] that [convicted child abuser Gerald] Amirault's sister, Cheryl Amirault LeFave, should be granted a new trial on her conviction of sexual abuse because of new scientific findings.

"Overzealous and inadequately trained investigators, perhaps unaware of the grave dangers of using improper interviewing and investigative techniques, questioned these children and their parents in a climate of panic, if not hysteria, creating a highly prejudicial and irreparable set of mistakes," the judge wrote. "These grave errors led to the testimony of the children being forever tainted."

Prosecutors maintain that the Amiraults got fair trials, and the state supreme court has repeatedly ruled against the family. But the court has never dealt with a lower court ruling like Judge Borenstein's.

Judges elsewhere, however, have previously cited suggestibility research in overturning a ruling made when it was all but given among clinicians—based more on gut instinct than data—that children would never lie about sexual abuse. The research played a role in a New Jersey appeals court's 1993 decision to free Margaret Kelly Michaels, who was convicted in 1988 in the Wee Care case, and has figured in other rulings and verdicts. The Michaels decision noted that "certain questions planted sexual information in the children's minds."

Carey Goldberg, "Getting to the Truth in Child Abuse Cases: New Methods," *New York Times*, September 8, 1998.

Document 11: Child Abuse and Violent Behavior

Michael J. Sniffen reports that a Justice Department survey found that a third of female prison inmates were abused as children, suggesting strong links between childhood abuse and adult behavior.

WASHINGTON—More than a third of the women in state prisons and jails say they were physically or sexually abused as children, roughly twice the rate of child abuse reported by women overall, the Justice Department said.

The figures for male inmates who suffered child abuse, while far smaller, also are about double that of the overall male population, according to a study by the department's Bureau of Justice Statistics.

More than 36 percent of female state prison and jail inmates surveyed in 1996–7 reported they were abused sexually or physically at age 17 or younger, the bureau reported.

By comparison, 16 studies of child abuse in the general population found that 12 percent to 17 percent of women were abused as children.

Among male inmates of state prisons, 14 percent suffered child abuse compared with 5 percent to 8 percent of the general male population, the bureau said.

"I'm not surprised," said Eleanor Smeal, president of the Feminist Majority Foundation. "While the inmate population is overwhelmingly male, the women who end up behind bars have had a very hard life."

"Childhood abuse increases the risk that anyone, female or male, could end up in prison, because the home influence is so pervasive," Smeal said.

"Women abused as children have their whole self-image changed. They believe they are bad. They end up in relationships with men who abuse them and in risky situations."

The survey also found alcohol and drug abuse was higher among inmates who suffered abuse than among those who did not.

Among state prison inmates, 80 percent of the abused women and 76 percent of the abused men regularly had used illegal drugs, compared with 65 percent of the women and 68 percent of the men who had not been abused.

Counting sexual or physical abuse at any age before imprisonment, the survey found nearly half of the women in prison, jail or on probation had been attacked, compared with 10 percent of the men in prison, jail or on probation.

This ratio of 5-to-1 may reflect simply the established fact that more women than men suffer physical or sexual abuse.

The survey found that a third of women in state prisons and a quarter of those in local jails said they had been raped before they were jailed. In state prisons and local jails, 3 percent of men reported they had been raped before incarceration.

Abused state prisoners were more likely than those not abused to have served time for violent crimes.

Among males, 76 percent of abused inmates, but only 61 percent of those not abused, had a current or past sentence for a violent offense. Among women, 45 percent of the abused, but only 29 percent of those not abused, had served a sentence for violence.

Prisoners reported higher levels of abuse if they grew up at least partly in foster care rather than with parents, if their parents were heavy drug or alcohol users or if a family member had been imprisoned. The study noted that many foster children had been removed from homes where they were abused by parents.

The study found little difference in the percentage of abused inmates growing up with one parent or those with two parents.

Michael J. Sniffen, "Child Abuse High for Female Inmates," *Journal*, April 12, 1999, www.jrn.com/news/99/Apr/jrn32120499.html.

Document 12: Child Protective Services Need Assistance

In this excerpt from a report to the U.S. House of Representatives, Jane L. Ross, director of income security issues in the Health, Education, and Human Services Division of the U.S. General Accounting Office, concludes that child protective services (CPS) face an increase in the problem of child abuse. Ross declares that CPS needs increased federal funding and aid in developing effective strategies.

Public agencies responsible for protecting children have faced increased reports of child abuse and neglect, as well as a disturbing increase in the number of families with severe and multiple problems. The high incidence of substance abuse found in these families places CPS caseworkers on the front line of one of our nation's biggest social problems. While the commitment of these workers to protect abused children is strong, the obstacles facing CPS units are daunting. A decade of calls for reform by national advisory boards and commissions has produced few improvements in many of the fundamental problems found in CPS units.

The burden to improve the ways CPS units respond to children at risk of abuse and neglect falls on state and local governments. However, the responsibility for the safety and well-being of a community's children cannot rest solely on an overwhelmed CPS system. CPS units have recognized that the traditional approaches to child protection cannot keep pace with the demand for services. CPS units are now reaching out to communities to establish partnerships among service agencies, attempting to share the responsibility for the safety of a neighborhood's children among a community's service providers, as well as its citizens, and increasing the attention given to support services. However, state child welfare officials responsible for CPS operations must not lose sight of the potential effect that long-standing systemic problems may have on these reform efforts. These officials must seek ways to correct deficiencies and to build and maintain the personnel and information systems that will support the new strategies. Without addressing these problems, reform goals may not be fully realized. In addition, state officials must be cautious about implementing new strategies for handling maltreatment reports, given the limited information available on their effectiveness.

A new era of federal partnership is needed to help CPS units respond to the rising rates of child maltreatment. While the federal government has funded research efforts on abuse and neglect, HHS [Health and Human Services] needs to better support the emerging needs of state and local CPS units. Local governments can ill afford to independently develop, test, and implement new strategies to protect our nation's children. New federal strategies are needed to provide focused assistance to CPS units and to evaluate and disseminate information about local efforts. Without federal assistance, states and localities will continue to find their own solutions to combat the problems of abuse and neglect, not benefitting from the collective experience of the entire nation.

Jane L. Ross, *Child Protective Services: Complex Challenges Require New Strategies*. Washington, DC: General Accounting Office, July 1997.

Document 13: The Strong Correlation Between Substance and Child Abuse

The National Association of Children of Alcoholics promotes awareness of the emotional, psychological, and developmental problems that children of substance abusers face. One of the organization's fact sheets, excerpted below, cites research showing that a large portion of child abuse cases involve parents who are alcoholics or exhibit other drug problems.

Seventy-six million Americans, about 43% of the U.S. adult population, have been exposed to alcoholism in the family. Almost one in five adult Americans (18%) lived with an alcoholic while growing up. . . .

Compared with non-alcoholic families, alcoholic families demonstrate poorer problem-solving abilities, both among the parents and within the family as a whole. These poor communication and problem-solving skills may be mechanisms through which lack of cohesion and increased conflict develop and escalate in alcoholic families. . . .

A significant number of children in this country are being raised by addicted parents. With more than one million children confirmed each year as victims of child abuse and neglect by state child protective service agencies, state welfare records have indicated that substance abuse is one of the top two problems exhibited by families in 81% of the reported cases.

Studies suggest an increased prevalence of alcoholism among parents who abuse children.

Existing research suggests alcoholism is more strongly related to child abuse than are other disorders, such as parental depression.

National Association of Children of Alcoholics, "Children of Alcoholics: Important Facts," August 1998, www.health.org/nacoa/impfacts.htm.

Document 14: Low Recidivism for Sex Offenders

In this excerpt from a report by the National Center on Institutions and Alternatives, the organization argues that the act of being caught is often such a shocking ordeal for sex offenders that they never repeat their crimes, and that this is shown in low recidivism rates for sex offenders.

It is well established that most sex offenders have histories of being molested themselves as children. This trauma leaves many of them with a long term problem of clouded boundaries. If the problem becomes deep seated enough, the victim may become a perpetrator. But with arrest and the other shocking consequences of being discovered, those uncertain boundaries are suddenly and vividly redrawn. For most, that drawing emerges with very hard lines.

More than with any other class of offender, getting caught leaves sex offenders humiliated, shamed and shaken to the core. Being handcuffed and hauled away from decent society is a shattering experience for anyone, but it is all the more electrifying and soul-stripping when the nature of the offense is as intimate and shameful a secret as is a sex crime. In some cases, the perpetrator's first real lesson in recognizing the consequence for his behavior comes with the shock of seeing his name and perhaps his picture in the newspaper or on television, accused and exposed before all his friends, family, neighbors, co-workers.

The process hardly ends with arrest. Prior to sentencing, which can sometimes take a year or more, little can be worse than the prolonged agonies and reflections of not knowing how long one may be going to prison, for some it may be for life. In this setting, life around them becomes narrow and terrifying. If pending trial, a sex offender is already bracketed in jail, it may be the first time his blurred boundaries come face to face with real vengeance. Greeted with beatings or worse, many first time sex offenders are startled by the degree of rage they now must encounter. Perhaps most devastating of all is the gradual realization that they are themselves criminals and as a known sex offender, the safety, comfort and security of the life left behind may be gone forever.

All of this is much more of a shock than putting a finger in a light socket, it is not just another passing experience. For sex offenders, more than almost any other class of criminal, being caught is the major crossroad in their lives. As with other forms of extreme aversion therapy, all of these humiliations imprint a painful, life-changing lesson. Few will ever forget the nightmare. As these low recidivism rates attest, getting caught teaches most.

National Center on Institutions and Alternatives, "Community Notification and Setting the Record Straight on Recidivism," November 8, 1996, www.igc.org/ncia/comnot.html.

STUDY QUESTIONS

Chapter 1

1. After reading Viewpoint 1 and Viewpoint 2, do you believe that the prevalence of child abuse is underestimated or exaggerated? What examples from the viewpoints support your own argument?

2. Viewpoint 3 suggests that children can act as reliable witnesses in child abuse cases. What factors would ensure a better understanding of the child's personal account? What other factors might boost the credibility of the testimony of child witnesses?

3. Early in Viewpoint 4, the image of a witch-hunt is presented. How is the image of a witch-hunt related to the phenomenon of false allegations? What examples from the viewpoint show similarities between witch-hunts and divorce custody cases?

4. What examples from the viewpoints are the most persuasive indicators of the extent of child abuse today? Which is more important to you in making your assessment: statistics from general studies or specific personal accounts? Why?

Chapter 2

1. Viewpoint 1 blames the changing structure of the American family for an increase in child abuse. Do you agree that families consisting of a married mother and father are less prone to child abuse than single-parent households? Explain your answer.

2. As indicated in Viewpoint 2, depression can cause parents to physically harm their children. What are some of the ways that depression can cause parents to neglect their children's needs?

3. Of the different causes of child abuse presented in this chapter, which do you think contributes most to the problem? What aspects of that viewpoint strengthen its argument?

4. The viewpoints in this chapter all discuss the role of parents in child abuse. What steps does each viewpoint recommend parents take in order to help prevent child abuse?

Chapter 3

1. Viewpoint 1 and Viewpoint 2 discuss the responsibilities and tasks of the child protection system. What responsibilities and powers do you think state child protective services should have? What agencies (social workers, law enforcement, legal professionals) do

you think should be most responsible for determining how to treat abused children?

2. Community notification laws, as discussed in Viewpoint 3 and Viewpoint 4, are active in every state. What are the advantages and disadvantages of these laws? How would you improve these laws?

3. After reading Viewpoint 5 and Viewpoint 6, which do you think is the best way to stop child molesters: punishment or rehabilitation? Support your argument.

4. The viewpoints in this chapter focus on the offender in strategies to reduce child abuse. How can children be more actively involved participants in reducing child abuse? Is it necessary that victims be recognized in discussions about reducing child abuse?

ORGANIZATIONS TO CONTACT

The editors have compiled the following list of organizations concerned with the issues debated in this book. The descriptions are derived from materials provided by the organizations. All have publications or information available for interested readers. The list was compiled on the date of publication of the present volume; the information provided here may change. Be aware that many organizations take several weeks or longer to respond to inquiries, so allow as much time as possible.

ACT for Kids
7 S. Howard, Suite 200, Spokane, WA 99201-3816
(509) 747-8221 • fax: (509) 747-0609
e-mail: info@actforkids.org • website: http://www.actforkids.org

ACT for Kids is a nonprofit organization that provides resources, consultation, and training for the prevention and treatment of child abuse and sexual violence. The organization publishes workbooks, manuals, and books such as *My Very Own Book About Me* and *How to Survive the Sexual Abuse of Your Child*.

American Academy of Child and Adolescent Psychiatry (AACAP)
3615 Wisconsin Ave. NW, Washington, DC 20016-3007
(202) 966-7300 • fax: (202) 966-2891
website: http://www.aacap.org

AACAP is a nonprofit organization that supports and advances child and adolescent psychiatry through research and the distribution of information. The academy's goal is to relieve the stigma associated with mental illnesses and assure proper treatment for children who suffer from mental or behavioral disorders due to child abuse, molestation, or other factors. AACAP publishes fact sheets on a variety of issues concerning disorders that may affect children and adolescents.

American Professional Society on the Abuse of Children (APSAC)
407 S. Dearborn, Suite 1300, Chicago, IL 60605
(312) 554-0166 • fax: (312) 554-0919
e-mail: APSACMems@aol.com

APSAC is dedicated to improving the coordination of services in the fields of child abuse prevention, treatment, and research. It publishes a quarterly newsletter, the *Advisor*, and the *Journal of Interpersonal Violence*.

False Memory Syndrome Foundation
3401 Market St., Suite 130, Philadelphia, PA 19104-3315
(215) 387-1865 • (800) 568-8882 • fax: (215) 387-1917
e-mail: pjf@saul.cis.upenn.edu

The foundation believes that many "delayed memories" of sexual abuse are the result of false memory syndrome (FMS). In FMS, patients in therapy "recall" childhood abuse that never occurred. The foundation seeks to discover reasons for the spread of FMS, works for the prevention of new cases, and aids FMS victims, including those falsely accused of abuse. The foundation publishes a newsletter and various papers and distributes articles and information on FMS.

Federation on Child Abuse and Neglect
134 S. Swan St., Albany, NY 12210
(518) 445-1273 • (800) 244-5373
website: http://www.childabuse.org (National Committee to Prevent Child Abuse website)

Created by the National Committee to Prevent Child Abuse, the federation is dedicated to preventing child abuse by raising public awareness about the causes and prevention of abuse. It also advocates legislation aimed to protect children from abuse. The federation offers brochures such as *What Kids Should Know About Child Abuse and Neglect*, booklets such as *Child Sexual Abuse Guidelines for Health Professionals*, fact sheets, and reprinted articles.

King County Sexual Assault Resource Center (KCSARC)
PO Box 300, Renton, WA 98057
(206) 226-5062 • fax: (206) 235-7422

KCSARC provides crisis intervention, counseling, consultation, and legal assistance to victims and survivors of child sexual abuse, incest, and sexual assault. The program also provides training for teachers, parents, and other professionals who work with children. KCSARC publishes the newsletters *Outlook* and *Teen Talk* as well as a variety of resources, including videos, books, and pamphlets.

National Center for Missing and Exploited Children (NCMEC)
2101 Wilson Blvd., Arlington, VA 22201-3077
(703) 235-3900 • fax: (703) 235-4067
hotline: (800) 843-5678
website: http://www.missingkids.org

NCMEC serves as a clearinghouse of information on missing and exploited children and coordinates child protection efforts with the private sector. A number of publications on these issues are available, including guidelines for parents whose children are testifying in court, help for abused children, and booklets such as *Children Traumatized in Sex Rings* and *Child Molesters: A Behavioral Analysis.*

National Clearinghouse on Child Abuse and Neglect Information
PO Box 1182, Washington, DC 20013-1182
(703) 385-7565 • (800) 394-3366 • fax: (703) 385-3206
e-mail: nccanch@calib.com
website: http://www.calib.com/nccanch

The clearinghouse collects, catalogs, and disseminates information on all aspects of child maltreatment, including identification, prevention, treatment, public awareness, training, and education. The clearinghouse offers various reports, fact sheets, and bulletins concerning child abuse and neglect.

National Coalition Against Domestic Violence (NCADV)
Child Advocacy Task Force
PO Box 18749, Denver, CO 80218-0749
(303) 839-1852 • fax: (303) 831-9251
website: http://www.ncadv.org

NCADV represents organizations and individuals that assist battered women and their children. The Child Advocacy Task Force deals with issues affecting children who witness violence at home or are themselves abused. It publishes the *Bulletin*, a quarterly newsletter.

National Criminal Justice Reference Service (NCJRS)
U.S. Department of Justice
PO Box 6000, Rockville, MD 20849-6000
(301) 519-5500 • (800) 851-3420
e-mail: askncjrs@ncjrs.org • website: http://www.ncjrs.org

NCJRS is a research and development agency of the U.S. Department of Justice established to prevent and reduce crime and to improve the criminal justice system. Among its publications are *Resource Guidelines: Improving Court Practice in Child Abuse and Neglect Cases* and *Recognizing When a Child's Injury or Illness Is Caused by Abuse.*

The Safer Society Foundation
PO Box 340-I, Brandon, VT 05733-0340
(802) 247-3132 • fax: (802) 247-4233
e-mail: ray@usa-ads.net • website: http://www.safersociety.org

The foundation is a national research, advocacy, and referral center for the prevention of sexual abuse of children and adults. The Safer Society Press publishes research, studies, and books on treatment for sexual victims and offenders and on the prevention of sexual abuse.

Survivor Connections
52 Lydon Rd., Cranston, RI 02905-1121
(401) 941-2548 • fax: (401) 941-2335
e-mail: scsitereturn@hotmail.com
website: http://www.angelfire.com/ri/survivorconnections/

Survivor Connections is an activist center for survivors of incest, rape, sexual assault, and child molestation. It publishes the *Survivor Activist*, a newsletter available by subscription.

United Fathers of America (UFA)
6360 Van Nuys Blvd., Suite 8, Van Nuys, CA 91401
(818) 785-1440 • fax: (818) 995-0743
e-mail: info@unitedfathers.com
website: http://www.fathersunited.com • http://www.fathersforever.com (a branch of UFA)

UFA helps fathers fight for the right to remain actively involved in their children's upbringing after divorce or separation. UFA believes that children should not be subject to the emotional and psychological trauma caused when vindictive parents falsely charge ex-spouses with sexually abusing their children. Primarily a support group, UFA answers specific questions and suggests articles and studies that illustrate its position.

Victims of Child Abuse Laws (VOCAL) National Association of State VOCAL Organizations (NASVO)
4584 Appleton Ave., Jacksonville, FL 32210

hotline: (303) 233-5321 • fax: (904) 381-7097
e-mail: vocal@vocal.org • website: http://www.vocal.org

VOCAL provides information, research data, referrals, and emotional support for those who have been falsely accused of child abuse. NASVO maintains a library of research on child abuse and neglect issues, focusing on legal, mental, social, and medical issues, and will provide photocopies of articles for a fee. It publishes the bimonthly newsletter *NASVO News.*

FOR FURTHER READING

Leory Ashby, *Endangered Children: Dependency, Neglect, and Abuse in American History*. New York: Macmillan, 1997. Outlines the history of abused American children from the colonial era to the present, focusing on the adult political agendas that have impacted children's lives.

Freda Ingle Briggs, *From Victim to Offender: How Child Sexual Abuse Victims Become Offenders*. Chicago: IPG Chicago, 1995. Stories of individual cases illustrate how victims of child sexual abuse go on to perpetuate the cycle of abuse. Argues for drastic changes to child protective services and utilization of innovative treatment programs.

Cynthia Crosson-Tower, *Understanding Child Abuse and Neglect*. 4th ed. Boston: Allyn & Bacon, 1998. An overview that focuses on the history of child maltreatment; family roles, responsibilities, and rights; sexual abuse; and foster care.

Howard Dubowitz, *Neglected Children: Research, Practice, and Policy*. Thousand Oaks, CA: Sage, 1999. A scholarly compendium of research and theory in treating neglected children. Includes essays on cultural aspects, fatalities, and alcohol and drug use.

Ellen Gray, *Unequal Justice: The Prosecution of Child Sexual Abuse*. New York: Free Press, 1997. Examines the legal aspect of investigating and prosecuting child sexual abuse, portraying how the criminal justice system sometimes mishandles the cases. Compares how the legal systems of different countries treat child sexual abuse.

Mic Hunter, *Child Survivors and Perpetrators of Sexual Abuse: Treatment Innovations*. Thousand Oaks, CA: Sage, 1995. Offers unique strategies for treating sexual abuse victims through interesting discussions about every major contemporary issue related to child sexual abuse.

Robin Karr-Morse, Meredith S. Wiley, and T. Berry Brazelton, *Ghosts from the Nursery: Tracing the Roots of Violence*. New York: Grove/Atlantic, 1999. Emphasizes the importance of the first few years of a child's life in healthy emotional development by tracing violent behavior back to abuse and neglect experienced in childhood. Offers case histories of problem children and reviews of research in brain development.

Anna J. Michener, *Becoming Anna: The Autobiography of a Sixteen-Year-Old*. Chicago: University of Chicago Press, 1998. A tragic story of a woman's abusive first sixteen years turns triumphant when she finds new legal guardians, personal growth, and a powerful voice to tell her story. Describes abusive parents, abusive workers at a mental institution, and steps toward recovery.

Keith N. Richards, *Tender Mercies: Inside the World of a Child Abuse Investigator*. Washington, DC: Child Welfare League of America, 1999. One child protection service worker's experience in New York, including investigating child abuse cases, interacting with abused children and abusive parents, and struggling with the bureaucracy.

Eric Shelman and Stephen Lazoritz, *Out of the Darkness: The Story of Mary Ellen Wilson*. Lake Forest, CA: Dolphin Moon Publishing, 1999. Story of the first abused American child to be removed from her home, resulting in a landmark case that established the foundations of modern-day child protection in the United States.

Jane Waldfogel, *The Future of Child Protection: How to Break the Cycle of Abuse and Neglect*. Cambridge, MA: Harvard University Press, 1998. Describes the troubling state of the current child protection services system and offers a reformed model in which the community can play a larger role in protecting children.

Kenneth Wooden, *Child Lures: What Every Parent and Child Should Know About Preventing Sexual Abuse and Abduction*. Arlington, TX: Summit Publishing Group, 1995. Provides a thorough guide for self-protection based on interviews with child molesters and murderers. Presents scenarios and explains common tricks molesters use, and suggests strategies for avoiding abuse.

WORKS CONSULTED

Books

Donald C. Bross, "The Legal Context of Child Abuse and Neglect: Balancing the Rights of Children and Parents in a Democratic Society," in Mary Edna Helfer, Ruth S. Kempe, and Richard D. Krugman, eds., *The Battered Child.* Chicago: University of Chicago Press, 1997.

Edward F. Dolan, *Child Abuse.* New York: Franklin Watts, 1992. Outlines different forms of child abuse and provides information on recognizing abuse and finding community resources for treatment.

Joan E. Durrant, "The Swedish Ban on Corporal Punishment: Its History and Effects," in *Family Violence Against Children: A Challenge for Society,* New York: Walter de Gruyter, 1996, pp. 19–25.

Ake W. Edfeldt, "The Swedish 1979 Aga Ban Plus Fifteen," in *Family Violence Against Children: A Challenge for Society.* New York: Walter de Gruyter, 1996, pp. 27–37.

Detlev Frehsee, Wiebke Horn, and Kai-D. Bussman, eds., *Family Violence Against Children: A Challenge for Society.* New York: Walter de Gruyter, 1996. A collection of research-based essays discussing family dynamics and possible solutions to child abuse.

Mary Edna Helfer, Ruth S. Kempe, and Richard D. Krugman, eds., *The Battered Child.* Chicago: University of Chicago Press, 1997. Outlines the latest advances in child abuse research. Proposes new techniques in assessment, treatment, and prevention of child abuse from various viewpoints, including medicine, law, and psychiatry.

Philip Jenkins, *Moral Panic: Changing Concepts of the Child Molester in Modern America.* New Haven, CT: Yale University Press, 1998. Explores the historical shifts in attitudes about child molestation and describes the social, political, and ideological influences that helped shape public opinion and governmental legislation on child molestation.

Karen Kinnear, *Child Sexual Abuse: A Reference Handbook.* Santa Barbara, CA: ABC-CLIO, 1995. A thorough and accessible overview of child sexual abuse, emphasizing personal stories and long-term effects.

Elaine Landau, *Child Abuse: An American Epidemic.* Englewood Cliffs, NJ: Silver Burdett, 1990. A readable overview of the many forms of child abuse. Includes case histories of battered children and information on relevant community organizations.

John R. Lutzker, ed., *Handbook of Child Abuse Research and Treatment.* New York: Plenum Press, 1998. Describes developments in child abuse research and treatment, emphasizing research studies and sociological issues.

Michael W. Weber, "The Assessment of Child Abuse: A Primary Function of Child Protective Services," in Mary Edna Helfer, Ruth S. Kempe, and Richard D. Krugman, eds., *The Battered Child.* Chicago: University of Chicago Press, 1997, p. 127–134.

Richard Weissbourd, *The Vulnerable Child: What Really Hurts America's Children and What We Can Do About It.* Reading, MA: Addison Wesley Longman, 1996. Explores aspects of contemporary culture that have a negative impact on children. Provides strategies for parents, schools, and various governmental agencies in protecting and supporting children.

Periodicals and Websites

Donna Alvarado, "Close-up: California Mandates Chemical Castration," *Seattle Times*, September 18, 1996, www.seattletimes.com/extra/browse/html/altcast_091896.html.

American Humane Association, "The Link Between Child Abuse and Domestic Abuse," *Child Protection Leader*, September 1994, www.yesican.org/articles/linkadv.html.

Vicki Ashton, "Worker Judgments of Seriousness About and Reporting of Suspected Child Maltreatment," *Child Abuse & Neglect*, June 1999, pp. 539–48.

Bill Backlund, "Imprecise Child Abuse Laws Do More Harm than Good," *Northwest News*, August 25, 1998, www.comzone.com/nwnews/nnissues/v16n16/ed2.html.

Matt Bai, "A Report from the Front in the War on Predators," *Newsweek*, May 19, 1997, p. 20.

Armin A. Brott, "A System Out of Control: The Epidemic of False Allegations of Child Abuse," *Penthouse*, November 1994, www.vix.com/men/falsereport/childabuse/brott94.html.

Center for Children in Crisis, "Incest: The Ultimate Betrayal," March 25, 1998, www.shadow.net/~cpt/.

"Child Molester Could Be Released," *Collegian*, April 3, 1996, www.spub.ksu.edu/issues/v100/sp/n123/ap-molesterrelease-17.html.

John F. Conway, "Child Homicide," *Canadian Family in Crisis*, January 25, 1995, www.vix.com/men/battery/studies/child-homicide.html.

Ulysses Currie, "New Law Puts Abused Kids First," *Journal*, May 5, 1999, www.jrnl.com/news/99/May/jrn144040599.html.

———, "Protection for Maryland's Most Vulnerable," *Washington Post*, May 16, 1999.

Lloyd deMause, "The History of Child Abuse," presented as a speech before the British Psychoanalytic Society in London, 1993, www.geocities.com/HotSprings/Spa/7173/ph-abuse.htm.

Kenneth A. Dodge, John E. Bates, and Gregory S. Pettit, "How the Cycle of Abuse Works," *Harvard Mental Health Letter*, May 1991, www.mentalhealth.com/mag1/p5h-abu3.html.

Electra Draper, "Dad Found Dead with Child, Had Kidnapped Her Before," *Denver Post Online*, January 30, 1999, www.denverpost.com/news/news0130d.htm.

Celia W. Dugger, "Tug of Taboos: African Genital Rite vs. American Law," *New York Times*, December 28, 1996.

End Physical Punishment of Children, "Spanking: Facts & Fiction," February 3, 1999, www.stophitting.com/spanking.htm.

Patrick F. Fagan, "The Child Abuse Crisis: The Disintegration of Marriage, Family, and the American Community," *Backgrounder*, published by the Heritage Foundation, May 15, 1997, www.heritage.org/library/categories/family/bg1115.html.

———, "How Congress Can Protect the Rights of Parents to Raise Their Children," *Heritage Foundation Issues Bulletin*, July 23, 1996, www.heritage.org/library/categories/family/ib227.html.

Nancy Faulkner, "Parental Child Abduction Is Child Abuse," presented to the United Nations Convention on Child Rights, June 9, 1999, www.prevent-abuse-now.com/unreport.html.

Caroline Fraser, "Suffering Children and the Christian Science Church," *Atlanta Monthly*, April 1995.

Robert E. Freeman-Longo, "Feel Good Legislation: Prevention or Calamity," *Child Abuse & Neglect*, February 1996, pp. 95–101.

Martin Galloway, "False Abuse Allegations," *Single Dad*, April 29, 1997, http://concernedcounseling.com/ccijournal/mofalseabuse.html.

Susan Gilbert, "Infant Homicide Found to Be Rising in U.S.," *New York Times*, October 26, 1998.

Sylvia Lynn Gillotte, "The Child Witness," in *Representing Children in Family Court: A Resource Manual for Attorneys and Guardians ad Litem*, published by the South Carolina Bar, November 4, 1997, www.childlaw.law.sc.edu/resourcemanual.

Carey Goldberg, "Getting to the Truth in Child Abuse Cases: New Methods," *New York Times*, September 8, 1998.

Tammy Hardiman, "Research Asks: Just How Reliable Are Children's Memories," *Memorial University of Newfoundland Gazette*, April 25, 1996, www.mun.ca/univrel/gazette/1995-96/April.25/or1-asks.html.

Chandra M. Hayslett, "Castration Remedies Problem of Sex Crimes," *Daily Beacon*, August 28, 1996.

Bob Herbert, "An Unending Tragedy," *New York Times*, February 26, 1998.

Judith L. Herman and Mary R. Harvey, "The False Memory Debate: Social Science or Social Backlash?" *Harvard Mental Health Letter*, April 1993, www.mentalhealth.com/mag1/p5h-mem3.html.

Jim Hopper, "Child Abuse: Statistics, Research, and Resources," July 24, 1998, www.jimhopper.com/abstats.

Jan Hunt, "Ten Reasons Not to Hit Your Kids," 1996, www.naturalchild.com/jan_hunt/tenreasons.html.

Cynthia A. King, "Fighting the Devil We Don't Know: *Kansas v. Hendricks:* A Case Study Exploring the Civilization of Criminal Punishment and Its Effectiveness in Preventing Child Sexual Abuse," *William and Mary Law Review*, April 1999, pp. 1,427–69.

Bob Kirkpatrick, "Recent Escalation in Child Abuse Charges Tied to Divorce," *The Men's Issues Page*, March 15, 1995, www.vix.com/pub/men/falsereport/commentary/ass-law-judge.html.

Jeremy Leaming, "Parents Ask Florida Court to Dismiss Child-

Abuse Charges," *Free!* October 27, 1998, www.freedomforum.org/religion/1998/10/27childabuse.asp.

Steven and Ellie Lee, *In Pursuit of Justice*, 1994, www.efn.org/~srl/justice.html.

Thomas L. Lester, "Sex Offender Facility Committed to Change and Rehabilitation," *Corrections Today*, April 1995, pp. 168–71.

Libertarian Party, "Libertarians Ask: Will Megan's Law Protect Politicians—or Our Children?" *News from the Libertarian Party*, August 29, 1997, www.lp.org/rel/970829-Megan.html.

Elizabeth F. Loftus, "Repressed Memories of Childhood Trauma: Are They Genuine?" *Harvard Mental Health Letter*, March 1993, www.mentalhealth.com/mag1/p5h-mem2.html.

Eric Lotke, "Sex Offenders: Does Treatment Work?" *Issues and Answers*, 1996, www.igc.org/ncia/sexo.html.

Dan Lungren, "Results: Safe Communities," *Megan's Law Report*, May 1998, http://caag.state.ca.us/megan/meganrpt.htm.

Moms Online, "Child Abuse and Neglect," March 5, 1990, www.momsonline.com.

Richard P. Morin, "Ross Cheit Seeks More Accurate Analysis of Child Molestation Data," *George Street Journal*, March 7, 1997, www.brown.edu/Administration/George_Street_Journal/cheit.html.

MSNBC News Services, "Sexual Abuse of Boys Underreported," March 11, 1999, www.msnbc.com/news/219683.asp#BODY.

National Association of Children of Alcoholics, "Children of Alcoholics: Important Facts," August 1998, www.health.org/nacoa/impfacts.html.

National Center for Policy Analysis, "Does Punishment Deter?" *NCPA Policy Backgrounder*, August 17, 1998.

National Center on Child Abuse and Neglect, *A Coordinated Response to Child Abuse and Neglect: A Basic Manual*. Washington, DC: U.S. Department of Health and Human Services, 1992.

National Center on Institutions and Alternatives, "Community Notification and Setting the Record Straight on Recidivism," November 8, 1996, www.igc.org/ncia/comnot.html.

National Clearinghouse on Child Abuse and Neglect Information, "What Is Child Maltreatment?" February 25, 1999, www.calib.com/nccanch/pubs/whatis.htm.

National Coalition for Child Protection Reform, "Introduction:

How the War Against Child Abuse Became a War Against Children," *Issues*, 1997, www.nccpr.org/issues/1.html.

———, "They 'Erred on the Side of the Child'—Some Case Histories," *Issues*, 1997, www.nccpr.org/issues/2.html.

National Coalition to Abolish Corporal Punishment in Schools, "Arguments Against Corporal Punishment," *Facts About Corporal Punishment*, October 20, 1998, www.stophitting.com/ facts_about_corporal_punishment.htm.

National Committee to Prevent Child Abuse, "Child Abuse and Neglect Statistics," April 1998, www.childabuse.org/facts97.html.

National Victim Center, *Victims' Rights Sourcebook: A Compilation and Comparison of Victims' Rights Laws.* Arlington, VA: National Victim Center, 1996.

"Nevada OKs Penalty for Witnesses Who Don't Report Child Abuse," *Los Angeles Times*, June 12, 1999

New Hampshire Task Force to Prevent Child Abuse, "A Short History of Child Abuse," *Resources*, July 16, 1998, www.grannet.com/nhtf/res-history.htm.

Yael Orbach and Michael E. Lamb, "Assessing the Accuracy of a Child's Account of Sexual Abuse: A Case Study," *Child Abuse & Neglect*, January 1999, pp. 91–98.

Mark Pendergrast, "First of All, Do No Harm: A Recovered Memory Therapist Recants," *Skeptic*, April 1995, p. 40.

Anthony J. Petrosino and Carolyn Petrosino, "The Public Safety Potential of Megan's Law in Massachusetts: An Assessment from a Sample of Criminal Sexual Psychopaths," *Crime & Delinquency*, January 1999, pp. 140–58.

Prevent Child Abuse America, *The Relationship Between Parental Alcohol or Other Drug Problems and Child Maltreatment*, September 1996, www.childabuse.org/fs14.html.

Sherry A. Quirk, "When Children Tell and No One Listens," *Facing the Issues: Grief and Mourning*, July 12, 1997, www.yesican.org/articles/childrentell.html.

Adriana Ramelli, "Sex Offenders Must Get Used to Public Scrutiny," *Honolulu Star-Bulletin*, May 31, 1997.

Tere Renteria, "Keep Sex Offenders Away from Children," *San Diego Union-Tribune*, July 17, 1997.

Henry Risley, "Is Your Neighbor a Sex Offender?" *Corrections Today,* August 1997, pp. 85–89.

Lynn Rosellinin, "When to Speak," *U.S News & World Report*, April 13, 1998.

Andrew Schneider and Mike Barber, "Children Hurt by the System," *Seattle Post-Intelligencer,* February 24, 1998, www.seattle-pi.com/pi/powertoharm/therapy.html.

Ivan Sciupac, "Woman Recounts Childhood Sex Abuse," *Journal,* May 25, 1999, www.jrnl.com/news/99/May/jrn48250599.html.

Hans Sebald, "Witch-Children: The Myth of the Innocent Child," *Issues in Child Abuse Accusations,* vol. 9, no. 3/4, Summer/Fall 1996, pp. 179–86.

Katherine Seligman, "Chemical Castration May Not Work, Cost a Bundle," *San Francisco Examiner,* September 18, 1996.

Sexual Assault Crisis Center of Knoxville, TN, "Child Sexual Abuse," May 27, 1996, www.cs.utk.edu/~bartley/sacc/childAbuse. html.

Judith Sheppard, "Double Punishment?" *American Journalism Review,* November 1997, http://ajr.newslink.org/ajrdoublepun.html.

Sharon Simone, "Salem, Massachusetts 'Day of Contrition,'" *Facing the Issues: Grief and Mourning,* January 14, 1997, www.yesican.org/articles/salem.html.

Michael J. Sniffen, "Child Abuse High for Female Inmates," *Journal,* April 12, 1999, www.jrn.com/news/99/Apr/jrn32120499.html.

Janice Somerville, "More Harm than Good," *American Medical News,* January 6, 1992, p. 99.

Murray A. Straus and Carrie L. Yodanis, "Corporal Punishment of Children and Depression and Suicide in Adulthood," in Joan McCord, ed., *Coercion and Punishment in Long-Term Perspective.* New York: Cambridge University Press, 1994.

Christopher Sullivan, "Jury Rejects Death Penalty for Susan Smith," *Detroit News,* July 29, 1995, http://detnews.com/menu/stories/12189.htm.

Laurel Swanson, "What the Research Says About Physical Punishment," *Positive Parenting,* December 1, 1998, www.extension.umn.edu/Documents/D/E/Other/6961_01.html.

Mike Tharp, "Tracking Sexual Impulses," *U.S. News & World Report,* July 7, 1997, www.usnews.com/usnews/issue/970707/ 7sex.htm.

Rick Thoma, "A Critical Look at the Child Welfare System: Caseworker Training," *Lifting the Veil*, June 27, 1998, http://home.rica.net/rthoma/training.htm.

Andrew Vachss, "Sex Predators Can't Be Saved," *New York Times*, January 5, 1993.

Ellen E. Whipple and Cheryl A. Richey, "Crossing the Line from Physical Discipline to Child Abuse: How Much Is Too Much?" *Child Abuse & Neglect*, May 1997, pp. 411–44.

Barbara Dafoe Whitehead, "Dan Quayle Was Right," *Atlantic Monthly*, April 1993, www.theatlantic.com/atlantic/election/connection/family/danquayl.htm.

Karl Zinsmeister, "Growing Up Scared," *Atlantic Monthly*, June 1990, pp. 49–66.

Reports

National Center on Child Abuse and Neglect, *Executive Summary of the Third National Incidence Study of Child Abuse and Neglect.* Washington, DC: U.S. Department of Health and Human Services, 1996.

Office of Juvenile Justice and Delinquency Prevention, *Battered Child Syndrome: Investigating Physical Abuse and Homicide.* Washington, DC: Office of Juvenile Justice and Delinquency Prevention, 1996.

——, *Child Neglect and Munchausen Syndrome by Proxy.* Washington, DC: Office of Juvenile Justice and Delinquency Prevention, 1996.

——, *Criminal Investigation of Child Sexual Abuse.* Washington, DC: Office of Juvenile Justice and Delinquency Prevention, 1997.

——, *Interviewing Child Witnesses and Victims of Sexual Abuse.* Washington, DC: Office of Juvenile Justice and Delinquency Prevention, 1996.

Jane L. Ross, *Child Protective Services: Complex Challenges Require New Strategies.* Washington, DC: General Accounting Office, July 1997.

C.T. Wang and D. Daro, *Current Trends in Child Abuse Reporting and Fatalities: The Results of the 1997 Annual Fifty State Survey.* Chicago: Prevent Child Abuse America, 1998.

INDEX

ABOUT THE AUTHOR

Henny H. Kim has worked as a freelance book editor at Greenhaven Press, as a staff writer for *Fiske's Guide to Colleges,* and as a production editor at Sage Publications.

M 8164-TN

16